Shadowed

Legacy

A traditional Victorian-era Gothic mystery in which orphaned saloon singer Genevieve Bonneau is brought back to the Louisiana plantation her father left years before. Once there, Genevieve must learn the hard lesson that family does not always mean love, nor home equate safety.

Janis Susan May

– Author's Revised Edition –

S~AB

SEFKHAT~AWBI BOOKS

With love to my sisters by choice:
Sally Mosley Bondi
Soila Rubio Canales
Marilyn Mathis Spaulding

and to CAPT Hiram M. Patterson, USN/Ret
the most wonderful man in the world
with all my love

Books by Janis Susan May
electronic and/or paperback format

The Avenging Maid
Family of Strangers
The Devil of Dragon House
Legacy of Shades
The Egyptian File
The Jerusalem Connection
Inheritance of Shadows
Lure of the Mummy
Timeless Innocents
Welcome Home
Miss Morrison's Second Chance
Curse of the Exile
Echoes in the Dark
Dark Music
Quartet: Four Slightly Twisted Tales
Lacey
Passion's Choice
The Other Half of Your Heart

Books by Janis Patterson

The Hollow House
Beaded to Death
Murder to Mil-Spec (anthology)

Books by Janis Susan Patterson

Danny and the Dust Bunnies (childrens)

Chapter One

Shooting a man wasn't my idea of how to end the day my father was buried, but Big Billy Johnson didn't give me much choice. After the last of the funeral revelers had finally staggered on their way and I was looking forward to some sleep, the door suddenly flew open again, snapping off the flimsy latch in which I had so foolishly trusted.

" 'Bout time they went home, Gene."

Big Billy Johnson was rightly named; a great hulking brute of a man, he was larger than any man in that mining camp—or any other camp I had ever lived in—and ever since we'd come to Three Mile Creek he had been following me with his eyes. Of course, since I was one of only three women in camp, that wasn't strange, but there was something in the quality of his stare that always frightened me.

"What are you doing here?" I asked in a voice that shook no matter how I tried to stop it.

He grinned, showing a mouthful of snaggled brown teeth. "I've come to stake my claim on you, afore any of those other buzzards get in ahead of me."

"And I have nothing to say about it?" I was stalling, backing up as if afraid; in reality I was trying to reach the cot that served as my bed.

His grin didn't alter, as if he found the idea of my questioning his advances unworthy of a second thought. He stepped past the ruin of the front door and started toward me, his eyes glowing with a predatory light.

My leg made contact with the rough wooden frame of the cot, and quick as a rattlesnake's tongue, I had the fancy pistol out from under the pillow and pointed at Big Billy's heart. There had once been two of these old-fashioned silver-covered pistols, relics from Pa's past, but he had lost one in a long-forgotten game and I had taken the other some time ago to protect myself. It hadn't been hard to convince Pa that he had lost it in another drunken game. He had been losing a lot by that time.

"Stop!" I shouted, my voice more secure now.

Big Billy didn't seem to care. He kept coming, and his eyes held an ugly glitter.

Taking a deep breath, I pulled the trigger and the ancient pistol fired, filling the tiny room with the reek of gunpowder. Through the stinging smoke I could see Big Billy clasp his shoulder and stagger, but he didn't fall. Now the look in his eyes changed from excitement to something that filled me with fear. That was the trouble with those old one-shot weapons; if that one shot didn't do the job, you were pretty much up the creek.

Suddenly there was someone else in the tiny room, someone as out of place in that shabby cabin at the end of the road in a small mining town as a creature from another planet. Dressed in finer broadcloth and linen than I had seen in a long time, he stepped carefully through the shattered door and lightly tapped Big Billy's shoulder with the silver knob of his cane.

"I don't think the lady desires your company," he said softly, and when Big Billy charged him with an animal roar, he didn't flinch the way every other man in Three Mile Creek would have done. Instead, he stood his ground and, smiling slightly, laid the stick alongside the shaggy head. Big Billy slid to the floor without a sound.

"You have strange friends, Miss Bonneau."

Not even his well-modulated voice could completely conceal the shadow of contempt. I winced under his cool gaze and wished that I were wearing something other than my well-worn, shapeless trousers and one of Pa's worn-out ruffled shirts. Of course, that was the purest of wishful thinking, for I had nothing else but the tawdry satin from the saloon and the sad-looking dress that had been Mother's best, saved more for sentiment than fit.

"You are Miss Genevieve Bonneau, are you not?"

He even pronounced my name right—Zheahn-vee-ehve. Only Mother and occasionally Pa had ever called me that; most of the residents in the various mining towns had even had trouble with the simpler pronunciation of Jen-ih-veeve. Long ago we had all given up on ever hearing anyone say "Bonneau" correctly, and over the years I had become used to being called Gene Bonner. To hear my name pronounced correctly was a distinct shock.

"Yes, I am."

"Well, so you can talk; it's a start at least." He was

looking at me the way cattlemen looked at stock, and suddenly I didn't feel any safer with him than I had with Big Billy Johnson. "Well, Miss Genevieve Bonneau, I have come to take you home."

Chapter Two

It was ridiculous, of course. I had no home. Except for the loving presence of my mother and, to a much smaller extent, my father, I had never had a home. But when my mother spoke of "home," she meant the place where she had grown up.

The town was called Furneaux, a small community in Louisiana composed primarily of stores and churches, existing mainly to serve the surrounding plantations. Like everywhere else in the South during those pre-war years, cotton was unquestioned king; bankers loaned against crops and deposited profits for cotton growers; storekeepers sold to the planters and their wives, always searching for something that the self-sufficient plantations did not themselves produce; preachers used the Bible to justify slavery and the rigid status code of the time to their smug congregations.

That same status code split the town in two. On one side were the neat houses of the bankers and preachers, mixed in with the town houses of the planters; on the other side of the invisible line so sharply observed that it might have been drawn in stone and brick was the other part of Furneaux, the part where my mother had lived. It wasn't as bad as the shanties down by the river, where the few free Negroes lived, though the wealthy people who lived on the north side of town seemed to think so. Here the houses were smaller and not so grand. The stores were full of staples instead of luxuries, and they catered to the poor white farmers, overseers and their wives, and the few white artisans of the area. There were only two stores—old Hoffritz's, that carried only the poorest kind of liquor and food, and the one that had belonged to my mother's family.

As a child, especially during the hard times, I had dreamed about that store. I had never seen it, of course, and Mother had never really talked about it, but it was easy to imagine a great emporium filled with every treasure a greedy little girl's heart could desire. In my dreams I would walk the aisles, taking whatever piqued my fancy, then run happily to join a whole group of laughing people who looked vaguely like me.

It wouldn't have been like that, no matter what my dreams. From the little Mother did say, I gathered that the brother who raised her was a stern, God-fearing man given to lay-preaching in which he delighted in the fire and brimstone awaiting those who strayed from the narrow path he deemed to be the right one. The rooms above the store into which he crowded his family were small and ugly, she said, and the store itself an uninteresting conglomeration of dull necessities. It was an unlikely setting to find a girl of Mother's blonde peaches and cream beauty, a beauty her brother denounced as a temptation of the devil.

Even Pa said that Mother was the prettiest girl in town but in a town like Furneaux, it didn't make any difference how pretty a girl was if she didn't have money and breeding. A pretty poor girl was regarded as sort of a mistake of nature, and people watched her carefully, somehow expecting her to behave worse than her less beautiful equals, so that when she at last proved them right, the entire town could sit back and bask in their smug self-righteousness.

My father had come from Furneaux too, but from the other side. Pa had all the breeding and money anyone could ever dream of, and a wild streak as wide as a summer sky. There was nothing he wouldn't dare, no bet he wouldn't take, and it was the talk of the town when he started courting the storekeeper's sister. The churchgoers and merchants decried Mother's associating with "that mad Bonneau boy," and the aristocracy—those who still spoke to the Bonneaus—pursed their lips at Pa's lowering himself to pay serious attention to a storekeeper's sister.

One night, unfortunately compelled to shoot some man who had had the audacity to accuse him of palming an ace, Pa had to decamp suddenly, and he decided to take my mother with him. They were married in the next town and set out simultaneously on the road of life and the road to California.

By the time the road to California got them there, the money Pa had brought had dribbled away in various games of chance or assorted whiskey barrels. Undaunted, he kept assuring Mother that he would soon be on the up side again, and sometimes he was. For a time. at least.

My early childhood memories are widely contrasting; when we were in the money, there were new clothes for everyone, a wonderland of toys for me, dinners in fancy restaurants, elegant hotels full of gleaming marble and polished brass. When it was all gone, the pretty new treasures disappeared one by one to finance a new stake. We left the elegant hotels by the back stairs in the dead of night and occasionally had to steal our supper from an unwatched garden.

Finally there were more downs than ups, and the pretty luxuries were a thing of the past. Pa gambled more, lost more, drank more, until one day in my ninth year he simply didn't come home again. We were living in a drab little town incongruously called Silver Bluff; any appreciable amount of silver had played out in the days of the forty-niners and the rough rolling land held no height that could be called a bluff. Pa had said it was named after a high-stakes poker game, but Pa was apt to relate anything to a poker game.

In a way, Pa's disappearance was a good thing for Mother. All the long wandering years of their marriage she had been little more than a ghost, a sad shadow tagging along behind him, taking fortune as it came and having little more to do than amuse and care for me. Then, with Pa gone, she knew she had to do something. There was no time to allow her the luxury of grief or self-pity, so she plunged right into work.

We were living in a little frame house at the wrong

end of the main street; it had only two rooms and a kitchen, but it was Mother's only asset. She turned it into a restaurant. At first the people of Silver Bluff came more out of charity than anything else, but after they tried Mother's mountain adaptations of Creole recipes, people started to come because they liked it.

The little restaurant prospered, and its name spread, which was enough to bring my father back from his wanderings. At first Mother was overjoyed. When he dressed up in his best and went with us to church, she was happier than I had ever seen her. Then the short happy time ended and the gambling and the drinking began again; there were fights and yelling, and one night my father disappeared ... along with six months' profit from Bonneau's.

In the ensuing years that little episode was enacted several times, but never again did I see the wonderful glow of happiness on my mother's face. Each time after Pa would disappear, she'd sigh, blink back tears, and say, "We mustn't judge him too harshly, Genevieve, my darling. When those demon spirits get ahold of him, he just can't fight them."

But as I got older, she said this less and less.

Actually, those last years she said less and less about everything, until she hardly said anything at all. Even now I remember with awe the work she did; not only in the restaurant, but seeing that we always had two dresses each and keeping the tiny shed that was our room neat and tidy. On top of that, she insisted that I go to school, and when I came home she gave me lessons in what seemed to me to be the most useless things—how to set a table with twelve pieces of silver and which piece to use first and how to hold a fan and how to speak properly.

I thought it all rather silly. One used a fan simply to get cool, and the way I spoke made my classmates laugh at me; as for twelve pieces of silverware! Everyone knew that was ridiculous. All anybody really needed was a spoon and a knife and a fork at most. Still, Mother insisted, and so I humored her, moving around the little pieces of wood on which she had written various incomprehensible things such as "oyster fork" and "butter knife."

Then, in my thirteenth year, Mother's health began to fail. Although I spent more time in the restaurant, and we had hired an old Negro widow as a helper, Mother refused to slow down. Mother was my entire world. Nothing could happen to her; I would not let myself believe that anything was wrong.

Mother believed it, though. One afternoon I came home early from school when she wasn't expecting me. Brother Matthew, the circuit rider who preached in Silver Bluff every three weeks, was sitting with her.

"You've got to write that letter, Miz Bonneau." He pronounced it "Bun-oh" in his husky, earnest voice. "It's the only fair thing for the girl."

Mother sighed. "I suppose you're right," she said heavily. The warped old floorboards creaked as she walked on them. Being outside the partially open window, I couldn't see her, but I knew exactly where she was going, across the room to her trunk. In it was the ragged receipt book she used to keep the accounts for the restaurant; besides her Bible, it was the only thing of paper we had in the house.

A letter? For my own good? I was dying with curiosity and probably would have stood outside that window for hours, hoping to hear more, had not Old Dolly, the enormous black woman who helped out in the restaurant, come around the corner of the house just then and pressed me into service setting tables for supper.

Some time later Brother Matthew left the house, and from his pocket protruded a thin edge of folded white paper. Mother never mentioned it to me, and after a few months of watching for some sort of reply, I gradually forgot the matter.

Then the ultimate tragedy occurred; ten days before my fourteenth birthday, Mother died. She had been ill for several days, and it was frightening how quickly she went once she finally let go. It was as if she simply faded away to nothing. I sat with her during those last days, hoping that perhaps she'd open her eyes and really see me once more, or call my name before she went. She didn't. Just once she murmured something that could have been "Anton."

Anton was Pa's name. It was the last thing she ever said.

When we had come to Silver Bluff, the good people of the town had snubbed Mother, not wanting to associate with a gambler's wife. When she died, the entire town turned out for her funeral, to stand beside me as my mother was placed forever in that cold, alien earth.

The town worried about what to do with me; they ignored the fact that I had been running the restaurant for the past few months and fully intended to go on doing so. No one listened to me, however, and various plans were made for my welfare, ranging from going to live with the Petries as a hired girl to going to the poor farm or maybe being sent to the State Normal School as a pupil-teacher.

They needn't have worried. The restaurant had been making money steadily for the last few months, and that was a signal that Pa would show up again soon. He did, some three weeks after Mother's funeral, looking very clean and very penitent, as he usually did when he came home broke. He knew Mother never ceased to hope he would change, and he preyed cruelly on her dreams.

I think Pa was genuinely grieved by Mother's passing, no matter what anyone may say. He stood for a long time at her grave, then came home and crawled into a bottle. He was never completely sober again in his life.

Of course, he wouldn't listen to my plans for staying in Silver Bluff and keeping the restaurant going. Silver Bluff was too small to contain a man of his scope, he declared; he was going to make a fortune; there was a whole world out there waiting to be conquered. It was bottle-talk, but I was powerless to stop it. He sold the restaurant and, almost as an afterthought, took me along with him.

That was the end of one life and the beginning of another. All the security I had known with Mother was gone; I never knew where we would be staying, if we would have shelter or even food. The only constant was that Pa would eventually come back drunk and, more often as time went on, broke.

My career as a saloon singer began quite by accident. Until then Pa had regarded me as an obligation to be taken care of, driven by some dim notion of duty or family to keep me with him—or perhaps he just liked knowing that there was one person in the world who would take care of him, who would do his laundry and cook for him and tuck him in when he was too drunk to stand. In any case, one night after Pa hadn't been back to the shack we shared for two days, I started to fear the worst and crept down to the saloon.

That in itself was no small feat, for there were no decent women in the tiny mining town of Spit-N-Holler, and any female caught out in the dark was considered fair game. I took along the single dueling pistol that was my constant companion when Pa was gone.

He had lost that night, lost disastrously, so much that he couldn't even pay his bar tab. The barkeep had scant patience with freeloaders, so to set an example he had tied Pa to the end of the bar to be jibed at and spit on by the other customers. None of my pleading touched his heart, assuming that he had one, and he declared that only the money due him would set Pa free.

Well, we hadn't any money. Nearly all that had been Mother's—the pitiful amount she left and the proceeds from the sale of the restaurant—had gone in the first poker game. Of course I had nothing of my own. When he was winning, Pa usually tossed me a few coins, but those had to be spent on things like fuel and food and once on a length of calico to make me a dress, since I had outgrown the last one I owned. Needlework was one of the things Mother had tried to teach me; but I was a poor pupil, and the length of calico was all but ruined. I was ashamed to wear it and after that stuck mainly to trousers and Pa's worn-out shirts.

Desperate to get Pa out of that dreadful place, I offered to work off the indebtedness. I suppose I had in mind sweeping or washing dishes or something of that order; I was shocked down to my shoes when the barkeep smiled and told me what he had in mind.

Compared to the fates that can befall young women in such rough, isolated places, I suppose I was fortunate, though anyone would have had a hard time convincing me of that then. The barkeep had a mind to hear some singing; he thought it would serve to pacify his rowdy clientele. There was a tawdry costume some girl had left long ago during Spit-N-Holler's more prosperous days. I cried as I put it on.

To this day I can remember that costume: sleazy pink satin with grayish petticoats that had once been red. Old as it was, it still smelled of sweat and cheap perfume. There was some jewelry that went with it, which I didn't wear. Mother had always disdained any jewelry except her wedding ring, even when Pa could afford to give it to her. The thought of having to wear a dress that showed my arms and shoulders as well as my legs almost up to the knee was bad enough without having to add jewelry to it.

Even now I blush to remember what I must have looked like in that outfit. Scrawny, brown from the sun, my dark hair skewed up into an uncertain chignon... Had there been any other female within a hundred miles, I probably would have been laughed off the stage.

As it was, I was a surprising success, probably due to that very novelty. Lacking a piano player, I took a battered tambourine onstage with me and launched into "Nellie, the Saloon Keeper's Daughter," a song Pa often wailed when in his cups. The normally boisterous saloon was absolutely silent while I quavered my way through the song, and then, as I finished, exploded with applause. A hailstorm of silver, both in nugget and coin, pattered around my feet and I scrambled ungracefully to pick it up.

Taking courage from that, I started to sing the only other song I knew that wasn't a hymn, a sad ballad called "Bereft of a Mother's Love." By the time I was finished, most of those hardened grizzled miners were unashamedly bawling, and the hail of silver was even heavier than before.

That was the beginning of my career as a singer. By the time I had sung both songs a dozen times and fragments of many more, I had almost more silver than I could carry. Of course, Pa took it all, all that was left after settling his bar bill and his gaming debts, but the tide in our household had certainly changed.

As we moved from town to town, I learned more songs, accumulated some more presentable costumes, and managed to earn enough to keep us both in reasonable comfort, even taking into account Pa's gaming. I realize what the popular concept of saloon singers is, and in some cases such distasteful titles are indeed deserved, but I never did anything to be ashamed of, other than show an unseemly amount of lower limb.

There were men who wished otherwise, but Pa was always there to prevent me from suffering that ultimate degradation. I don't know how much longer he would have been able to do so, however, for the years of dissipation had severely weakened his constitution, so much so that when a bout of influenza struck him late in the spring, he was dead within two days.

It was the opening Big Billy Johnson had been waiting for. He had come to Three Mile Creek two weeks before and had been watching me ever since with the single-minded stare of a predator. He probably would have had his way with me, too, despite that hole in his shoulder—my aim had been lamentably bad—had not the fair-haired stranger knocked him out just before telling me he had come to take me home.

Chapter Three

Home.

I knew the name of it, of course. Furneaux Township, Vieux Cadeau Parish, Louisiana. Mother had talked of it with a wistfulness that made me think of an outcast angel longing for heaven. There was another name, too, one she mentioned less often: *Maison des Ombres*. It meant House of Shadows, and Pa had grown up there. Mother had been to the old plantation house only a few times, and Pa seldom spoke of the distant past, so I had only a hazy picture of the house where my grandfather lived, the place where he wanted me to join him.

"My grandfather?"

It was the next morning. The fair-haired stranger, who introduced himself as Jonathan Eversleigh, sat across from me, the sun touching his head with a halo of pale gold. The night before he had taken over everything, arranging that Big Billy be taken to the barred cave the town used as a jail and given medical help. Then he'd given me a healthy dose of whiskey and had seemed surprised when I coughed and choked with revulsion. After that, he had ordered me to bed and gone away. I learned later that he had spent the night on the cabin's rickety front porch, tipped back in the creaky old chair with his feet propped up on the rail, just in case there should be further trouble.

"Louis Philippe Montreaux Bonneau. Your grandfather. He asked me to find you. And your father, of course. A pretty chase you've led me."

"Why, Mr. Eversleigh?"

He looked surprised. It occurred to me that it must be very rare for anyone to question any action of Louis Philippe Montreaux Bonneau—a thought that was later confirmed.

"Why, Miss Bonneau? Why what?"

"My father left his home almost twenty years ago. I cannot believe you have been searching for us ail that time. Therefore the question is, why has he decided to seek us now?"

His eyes narrowed, and for one moment I felt a thrill of danger. The men in the mining camps were mainly simple brutes, controlled by force of personality or the threat of my trusty pistol; I had had several strained times, but I had never felt a sense of potential danger as I felt at that moment. Jonathan Eversleigh was a man the likes of which I had never met before.

"Your grandfather is getting old. He wants to set some things aright before he dies."

"Fence mending."

"I suppose. Sort of."

I nodded slowly. Somehow the idea of deathbed repentance didn't seem in keeping with the arrogant, strong-willed patriarch my mother had described, but since he had opposed her marriage to my father, I supposed she carried a prejudice against him. Pa had never mentioned his father that I remembered, nor any other member of his family except his sister, Felicité. She had been just coming into womanhood when he left, and to my knowledge she was the only relative he had ever contacted after that hurried midnight departure from the *Maison des Ombres*.

"Of course, the old man will be grieved to know of your father's death. He had hoped ..." Jonathan Eversleigh shrugged, his broad shoulders straining the fabric of his jacket.

At first I had thought him ugly. His face was strong, with harsh bones and well-defined features, but there was a purity of line, a strength that gave him a sort of beauty. Only the cold flashes that occasionally illuminated his eyes spoiled the image of a strong man on a charitable errand and made me reluctant to give him my trust.

Trusting or not, I had almost shocked myself with my behavior. Instead of my usual costume of breeches and shirt, I had chosen to receive him that morning in Mother's old go-to-church dress, which I had carefully preserved. It had never fit too well, for Mother had been much more daintily built than I, but only after it was too late did I realize how distressingly tight it was across the bosom. The skirt was so short it came well above my ankles, and I was forced to stay seated to hide that fact; however, the material was a dove gray trimmed with a touch of black braid and the neckline modestly high, so I felt safe in wearing it.

That is, I did until Jonathan Eversleigh actually entered the room, and then it wouldn't have made any difference what I wore. His cold green eyes dismissed my pathetic attempt at gentility, stripped away the gray dress as if it had never been, and seemed to bore deeply into my soul. It was a very uncomfortable feeling. Small wonder I thought Jonathan Eversleigh a man of whom I should be wary.

I thought of the years of deprivation and of my parents' sufferings, and a great wave of resentment grew about the old man of whom I had so seldom heard or thought. "It is a great pity he did not hope earlier."

"You are very young to be bitter."

"Bitter? I didn't mean to sound so. I am merely being honest."

His eyes clouded. "They are sometimes the same thing. Well, Miss Bonneau, are you prepared to return to Louisiana with me?"

I looked around the shabby cabin that was so like the other shabby cabins where we had lived, never with more possessions of our own than would fit into a carpetbag or two, and my answer was an instantaneous "Yes."

"Very well. First of all we must get you some decent clothes."

In spite of myself I blushed, and there was a ghost of laughter in his voice.

"I should think that you could wear your pants and shirt until we get to Denver." He cast a withering eye over my attire. "I doubt if there's anyone there who knows the Bonneaus."

The imputation that I should be an embarrassment to the Bonneaus—and how strange to think that there were more of that name than I!—angered me more than a little. "I shall endeavor to preserve the family's good name," I answered waspishly, "and if anyone asks, I shall say I know nothing of them."

At that he looked at me somewhat strangely and I wondered if my unwomanly tongue had gotten me in trouble, as Pa had always said it would. Of course, to Pa my tongue was always unwomanly whenever it disagreed with him.

"I suppose you can ride?"

I thought of the twisting track that was the only way into this town and wondered just how he thought I had gotten here, but kept my reply civil. "Yes, I can ride."

"Very well. Can you be ready to leave in the morning?"

In truth, I could have been ready in half an hour, but he seemed to think that a woman would need waiting for, and I would have hated to have him report to my unknown relatives my total lack of feminine sensibilities.

No, that's not quite true. At the time I took him for what his clothes proclaimed him to be—a dandy, unsuited to the ways of the West despite his skill with that cane—and did not relish the idea of the long trip down the mountain with a greenhorn; from Three Mile Creek down to the main road was a good day's ride. If we left right then, we would have to accomplish at least half the trip in darkness. Even though there was a goodish moon, I could not see picking my way down with him in tow.

By the next morning it was obvious that he had an equally low opinion of my abilities, for although he rode a sturdy gray horse, he was leading Jeb Hall's spavined old mare, which any two-year-old could have ridden safely. He even apologized that he had been unable to locate a sidesaddle. That was all right with me, for although I had heard of them, I had never seen one.

The rest of our trip was no better. We seldom spoke, even when we made camp that night. Apparently Mr. Eversleigh was taciturn by nature, while I was merely exhausted. Usually I am a good rider, but the strain of a day in the saddle after several weeks' absence, coupled with the effort necessary to keep Jeb Hall's old mare up to an amble, left me both disgusted and tired. We ate our beans in silence and rolled up in blankets on opposite sides of the fire.

"I hope you are not too uncomfortable, Miss Bonneau. I had hoped to find lodging for tonight."

I bit back the impulse to tell him that there would have been lodging available had he gotten me a horse that would move above a walk or any number of other interesting things about which I could have informed him had he but allowed me in on his plans. Unfortunately, however, I had already shown a hasty tongue, and I wished to present as good an impression on this emissary of my unknown family as possible.

"I am not uncomfortable, Mr. Eversleigh. Sleeping in

the open is not a new experience for me." Indeed, when Pa had been out of funds, we had often slept outside, and the weather had not always been as clement as this. No, this was not a new experience at all.

He was silent for a moment, then spoke up, "There is no need to recount this incident to anyone in New Orleans." Mr. Eversleigh had informed me that we would stop in New Orleans before going on to *Ombres*, as he called it.

"Don't worry; I shan't accuse you of maltreatment for failing to procure me lodging."

Incredibly, he laughed. If I had ever thought about such a thing, that dark rolling sound was just the laugh he should have. "That, Miss Bonneau, was not my worry. I care nothing for anything that sad band of leftovers and malcontents may say about me. It was you and your reputation I had in mind."

"My reputation?" I asked, somewhat shocked. I knew that being a saloon singer was considered quite risqué, but short of shooting Big Billy Johnson and of doing it so badly, I had done nothing of which anyone should be ashamed.

"Yes, Miss Bonneau, your reputation. Don't you know that just the hint of your having spent a night unchaperoned while under my protection could ruin you forever?"

No, I hadn't had the slightest idea of such a thing; after all, I seemed to be a great deal safer with this Jonathan Eversleigh than I would have been with Big Billy Johnson. If he were so bad, why had he been sent for Pa and me? I fell asleep worrying about that one.

For all my worries, our trip was singular only in its uneventfulness. In Denver Mr. Eversleigh set about arranging things with grim efficiency. I was installed in a hotel, quite as fancy as the best I had enjoyed in my early childhood, and kept virtual prisoner there while an army of insufferable females swarmed over me, smothering me in lace and muslin and heaven only knew what else. When they were through with what they snidely called the "bare minimum," I was covered in enough material to clothe half of Three Mile Creek. When I protested, Mr. Eversleigh merely laughed and said that it was just a foretaste of what would await me in New Orleans. Occasionally, during that awful day, I would catch him smiling.

He did have a devastating smile. During our trip down the mountain I had seen precious little but the back of his head and it had not been an occasion for smiling; however, seen straight on, one of those quicksilver grins lightened his grim, rather haughty face into a mask of charm.

The sewing ladies liked it. At least one of them was always in the living room of our suite, simpering while she asked his opinion of this or that. They seemed to resent the time they had to spend pinning garments on me, which might account for the way some of them looked; nothing so bizarre as the clothes some of them wore could be called pretty, let alone fashionable! I was to learn later how mistaken that idea was.

Lest there be some misunderstanding, be assured

that when I said "our suite," I did not mean Mr. Eversleigh's and mine; from the moment of our entry into Denver, he had been obsessed with propriety. By some magic he produced a very sedate, very proper, and very dull lady who was more than happy to earn her passage to New Orleans by playing gracious chaperone to a heathen barbarian.

Mrs. Wooley was the widow of a minister who had died of a fever contracted while attending to the spiritual needs of his flock. Widowhood is a sad, horrible thing and even more so when the details of its cause are repeated in detail at least twice a day. I quickly tired of hearing her lament, but at least it was preferable to enduring her lectures on genteel behavior. I had never heard anything so dismal in my entire life. Even Mr. Eversleigh's taciturnity was preferable, despite my distrust of his facile, mercurial charm.

Not that I had much choice. Having found me and attended to my needs, Mr. Eversleigh seemed intent on spending as little time with me as possible. When we traveled by coach, he rode separately, on horseback.

"No doubt looking out for savages," said Mrs. Wooley with a sigh, before launching into a lecture about the spiritual plight of the unconverted heathen.

When we switched to the railway, Mr. Eversleigh still avoided our company, always seeking space in another car.

"How considerate!" gushed Mrs. Wooley. "Doubtless he knows that ladies find cigar smoke offensive. No matter how good a man is at heart, he will hang onto his little vices."

I had my own opinion of Mr. Eversleigh's reasons for keeping his company to himself, but by the time we had reached the steamy heat of Louisiana, I had decided that whatever propriety said, cigar smoke was infinitely preferable to another hour of Mrs. Wooley's unending platitudes, homilies, and nauseating piety. Pleading a need to walk, if only along narrow aisles, I left Mrs. Wooley happily blathering about my understandable excitement at being so near to home at last and slipped away.

Mr. Eversleigh was in the third car back. It was not as luxuriously appointed as ours, but somehow I found the plain varnished wood more pleasant than dusty red plush and fringed velvet curtains.

"Miss Bonneau! Is there anything wrong?"

Without waiting to be asked, I sat down. "There is nothing wrong, Mr. Eversleigh. Must something be wrong for me to seek out your company?"

He was regarding me with that strange look again, as I might regard an animal of uncertain disposition and questionable reputation. "I should think you have enough of my company, Miss Bonneau. We see each other quite often."

It was true; he ate every meal with us, during which he made polite and trivial conversation with Mrs. Wooley, and he was always careful to see us comfortably situated, but we had not spoken alone together since entering the hotel in Denver. If I had been of a suspicious disposition, I might have thought he was avoiding me;

however, that may have been just because I wanted so desperately to talk to him.

"But always in the presence of Mrs. Wooley."

His thin lips twisted into a wry smile. "And you would wish it otherwise?"

Perhaps he intended to shock me; well, perhaps that might bring a blush to the gentle cheek of a sheltered Southern girl, but I was made of sterner stuff. "Most definitely. Why else do you think I came in search of you?"

The smile exploded into laughter. "By God, Miss Bonneau, I hope you learn to curb your tongue. Honesty is not well-favored in fashionable circles."

"Then I wonder that anyone should bother with them," I said dismissively. "Do you refer to my family?"

"I prefer not to discuss your family." A note of ice I had not heard before coated his voice.

"You are not playing fair with me, Mr. Eversleigh. You must know my relations, else they would not have entrusted to you the task of finding my father and me. Until a few days ago I was not even sure I had a family; now I am expected to join them, sight unseen. Is it any wonder I wish to know something about them?"

He regarded me for a long minute, his strange green eyes narrowed. Many times I had seen an expression like that around a poker table, gauging the odds, trying to read the other fellow's hand. Such unwinking scrutiny was unnerving, and I felt almost as if he were accusing me of holding something— *what?*—back.

"You have a point," he conceded, and I pressed my

advantage.

"Tell me of my family, Mr. Eversleigh."

"Very well, Your grandfather is not well, but don't think you will find an amiable doddering old man. His body may be weak, but his mind and his will are as strong as ever. He never leaves *Ombres* anymore."

I felt an involuntary thrill of excitement at the name: *Ombres*. It had such an air of glamour and mystery about it.

Maison des Ombres.

House of Shadows.

Home?

"He maintains the town house in New Orleans, of course, for your Aunt Felicité and Cousin Charlotte. He takes care of them since Felicité's husband was killed in the War." His voice changed sharply and, in response to my questioning glance, he added, "Your aunt and I are not fond of each other. That's really about all the family, except for Rouben. He's your uncle. Probably he would have been the best of the bunch if ..."

"If?"

"If there hadn't been a war. Damn fool that he was, he went to fight. There was never a man less suited to fighting, but he had some wild idea about honor and duty and beliefs. He was never the same after." Jonathan Eversleigh's expression as he turned to look out the window warned me not to question him further on the subject.

I knew about the War, of course. Its horrors had barely touched our western mountains, but when the dreadful conflict between North and South had ended the leftovers of the war, the sad men, the lost men, the broken men, had drifted to the West, seeking new lives but unable to forget the old. I had been barely ten when the War ended; Mother had grieved over it, and as I had come to know those displaced by its fury, I had come to hate its senseless waste.

"And you, Mr. Eversleigh? How do you fit into the family?"

"As little as possible, Miss Bonneau. As little as possible."

Chapter Four

I thought I was going to die.

The night before, I had thought my discomfort due mainly to fatigue and the rigors of travel; this morning I knew it was not. Having lived in the mountains most of my life, I was used to cool temperatures even in the summer. The muggy heat of New Orleans was an ugly surprise.

We had arrived late, so late that the family had already retired. The houses were strange, closed buildings that I would not have thought to be houses at all, but Mr. Eversleigh, moving with the surety of experience, directed the carriage to a tall, closed door in a seemingly solid wall and pounded until a sleepy Negro opened it.

It took him some talking to persuade the servant to admit me, and before I was allowed in, a tall, angular Negress had to be called to inspect me. By that time I was so tired and sleepy I ignored the insult; for the promise of a bed and some sleep, I would have tap-danced in the street.

Apparently I proved acceptable, for she beckoned me in, raising a cautious finger as a signal for silence. I bid a hasty and, I'm afraid, not very grateful farewell to

Mrs. Wooley, and another, scarcely less curt, to Jonathan Eversleigh, then blindly followed the woman in hope of a bed.

The bed itself was, by the light of day, quite the most luxurious I'd ever seen. Enveloped in a swirl of mosquito netting, I first thought I had awakened inside a cloud. The sheets, though thin with age and well darned, were of fine monogrammed linen. The furniture was heavily carved and substantial. On the washstand there were a matching bowl and pitcher of painted china and on the dresser a set of jars and pots and bottles in the same pattern. I had never seen such luxury even in the best of those dimly remembered hotels.

At first I thought I had awakened early, for the room was dim, but then I saw that there were shutters over the windows and beyond that the glitter of sunshine.

I leaped from the bed, fighting my way free of the enshrouding mosquito netting. What would my new family think of my lying abed so long? It was scarcely mannerly.

There was a bell pull on the wall; I yanked it and struggled into my nightgown. Perhaps it is an indication of an immodest nature, but the night before, I had slept in nothing but my bare skin. The muggy heat had made even the feeling of the sheets beneath me distasteful. Well, what I did in my own bedroom was my business, but I could not greet a servant so. The voluminous folds of thin cotton—which had seemed so ridiculously flimsy in Denver—settled around me like smothering blankets.

I needn't have hurried. It was fully ten minutes

before there was a knock on my door as it swung open. I never was to get used to the habit Southern servants have of knocking on their way in instead of requesting permission to enter; later I found that everyone else seemed to take it as a matter of course.

"Good morning, *Mademoiselle* Genevieve." It was the woman from the night before. In the light of day she was even more imposing than she had been by torchlight. Her skin was the color of burnished copper, not unlike that of some Indians, and her chiseled face was coldly arrogant. Only her walk marred the impression of some savage queen mysteriously placed into servitude; it was rolling, lurching, its ungracefulness indicating that somewhere under her old-fashioned circular hoops one leg was vastly different from the other.

"Good morning."

The tray she carried held a flaky pastry and a cup of steaming hot chocolate. I was hungry—dinner the night before had been both early and skimpy—but the sight of the hot chocolate almost killed my appetite. Already I was sticky and sweaty.

"I am called Agnes. This is your *petit dejeuner*. Are you ready for your bath?"

Bath? Lukewarm water ... it sounded wonderful. "Yes."

"I will have it drawn while you eat."

To my surprise, the hot chocolate was quite refreshing and the pastry—a croissant, as I would learn to call it—most enjoyable. Less pleasurable was the frozen-faced Agnes attending me at my bath. I had naturally expected her to leave, but she did not, and I had no idea of how to ask her. So I splashed about in the great metal tub, which, along with several large cans of water, had been carried up by a surprising number of strong young servants. There was a screen around the tub, but Agnes stayed on my side of it until I finished, then draped an enormous towel around me and handed me, one by one, almost every undergarment I owned.

I made no comment and put everything on. Obviously things were very different here in Louisiana, and if I were going to live here as I dreamed of, I would have to learn and conform.

It was going to be difficult, though; there were pantalets down to my ankles and a chemise and a corset and a corset cover and a multiplicity of petticoats. Even though my arms were bare, I had on more clothes than I had ever worn in my life! My old shapeless trousers and Pa's ragged shirt—both determinedly saved from destruction and now safely packed in the bottom of my valise—seemed desirable by comparison. I wondered if I should ever wear them again.

I smiled wryly and wondered what my new family would say if I should walk into their midst in my usual garb; would they react with pity, or scorn, or laughter? Somehow it seemed important to know, for it would be a clue to the kind of people they were, and that was something I wanted desperately to know. Mr. Eversleigh had been maddeningly vague about my family, completely immune to my pestering him for information. Could he not understand what it meant to me?

Obviously not, since he had said very little beyond the barest facts. I had been furious with him and, had I any idea that blows and angry words would have had an effect on that graven countenance, would have flown at him like a virago. All night I had alternated between trying to conjure up a picture of my unknown family from his scant information and thinking of scathing things to say to the uncommunicative Mr. Eversleigh!

I gasped for breath as Agnes pulled the strings of my corset tight. "Good heavens!"

"Exhale again, please, *mademoiselle*."

"Must I?" I already felt like a calf roped and tied for branding.

"Just a little more, *mademoiselle*. We will not try for too much today," she said with resignation.

Would my family be as demanding and as disapproving as Agnes? Somehow I feared they would, and that frightened me. I wanted so very much for them to like me. Morning had brought a strange charity for Mr. Eversleigh; apparently he had always known the security of a family, of knowing who his people were, and therefore could not understand the longing of one who had always been the outsider, the lonely one. As a child I had dreamed of a family like those seen occasionally— great knots of people bound by blood; grandparents, aunts and uncles, cousins, nieces and nephews, brothers and sisters. Someone like Jonathan Eversleigh could never understand my longing to be a part of the group, to be one who belonged instead of one who was asked for a meal or a ride or a visit just out of charity.

I could not even picture them. Would they be tall, like Pa? Dark, like Pa and me, or angelically fair? Had my unexpected talent for music been a Bonneau trait? Would they welcome me or...?

That was silly. They had sent all the way across the country for me, so they must want me.

"Is my family waiting for me?" Finally I had to ask; Agnes volunteered nothing.

"They are dressing now, *Mademoiselle* Genevieve. Breakfast will be served in the courtyard in an hour. You will meet them then."

"Breakfast? I thought ... "

"That was *petit dejeuner*. It is always brought when you ring in the morning." Her tone implied that it usually happened much earlier.

"And when will breakfast be?" I asked meekly.

"At ten, *mademoiselle*. Some thirty minutes from now. If you like, I shall come for you and help you into your dress." The last was said grudgingly, and I could not decide if it was a favor to me or a ploy to be sure I stayed put.

"Yes, please. Oh," I added suddenly as she turned to go, "could you please open the shutters? It looks like such a lovely day outside."

She didn't pause on her way to the door. "But that is forbidden, *Mademoiselle* Genevieve."

"Forbidden?"

"During the summer, yes. If the shutters were opened, the heat would become unbearable. Also, *Madame* deMarchand does not want the furnishings faded. Of course, usually at this time of year this house is closed." There was no doubt that somehow such disruption was all my fault, as in truth it was.

I waited until she left and the sound of her footsteps in the uncarpeted hall had died away before opening the shutters myself. Perhaps it might get hot later—and it was hot enough now—but I could not bear sitting in a closed-up room like some sort of night animal. With the shutters open, the room flooded with light and I could see that by afternoon the heat could become unbearable. Very well, I would close them again before the supercilious Agnes came to get me, but for now I wanted to see as much of my new surroundings as possible.

Cautiously, I peeked out from between the thin organdy curtains. Although it was styled for use as a window, the shuttered aperture could also be used as a door, leading onto the narrow balcony that ran all the way around the inside of the building. The house itself was hollow, built around a small courtyard alive with trees and plants. One aged giant in particular must have antedated the house by at least a century, for it not only cleared the roof but threatened to come right inside my room unless trimmed regularly. At varying intervals around the second-floor balcony were other doors like mine, all sensibly shuttered against the heat. Overhead the sky was an unbroken burning blue.

At one end of the courtyard was a solid wall, interrupted only by the door through which I had entered the night before. Now I could see that it was two doors in one—a large double one, big enough to admit a carriage and team, in which was set a small, person-size one. At the other end of the courtyard, almost under my window, was a large porchlike affair built out over the grass and flagstones.

"Kitty?"

1 jumped, first because I was startled, then again because I was frightened. The apparition standing not six feet away down the balcony, its arm waving wildly in my direction, was like no other human I had ever seen.

At one time he must have been an extraordinarily handsome man; now, however, the right side of his face was a horror of glazed purple flesh and twisted muscles. The eye was gone, though a flap of bluish skin had been crudely pulled down to cover the socket. No hair grew on that side of his head, and where the ear had been …

Yes, all of that was pathetic, but the really dreadful thing was that his other eye—china-blue and undamaged—was as devoid of intelligence as the vacant socket of the other one would have been. This poor creature had been hideously mangled, and his mind had been irrevocably destroyed.

Compassion overcoming fear, I smiled gently and held out my hand, wondering just who this could be; to roam free in the house, he would have to be close to the family, but nothing had been said about a cripple. Then my stomach lurched into a painfully tight knot, and with unquestionable clarity I knew why Mr. Eversleigh said my Uncle Rouben had never been the same after the War. No wonder he hadn't wanted to explain further.

"Kitty?" the pathetic creature repeated piteously,

pointing into the branches of the enormous tree. He pointed with his left hand; the right was tucked deeply into his coat pocket.

Following his finger, I could see a tiny yellow kitten clinging pathetically to a branch; although it was barely out of arm's reach from the balcony, the animal was a dizzying height above the stone-flagged end of the courtyard.

"Do you want your kitten, Rouben?" I asked, touched by his distress.

"Kitty?" His voice was tragic.

I should have called a servant; I should have looked for help; I probably should have done a number of things besides what I did, which was look quickly to see if there was anyone else around. Seeing no one, I skinned out of my voluminous petticoats and stepped out onto the balcony. This isn't as risqué as it sounds, for with the exception of my uncovered arms, my camisole and pantalets covered me quite as modestly as my old trousers and shirt had ever done.

"Kitty?"

"Just a minute, Rouben," I said as I would to a child. Perhaps he was my uncle and my senior, but he would never be more than a child.

Though it had been quite a while since I had sneaked away from Mother's overseeing eye to climb trees with the Crawford kids, I still remembered how to go from branch to branch without losing my balance. Being able to step directly from the balcony into the thickest part of the tree made it even easier.

The poor kitten was too terrified to run from me, but she definitely did not like being plucked from her airy perch. Teeth and claws flailed, and the only way I could keep from being cut to pieces was to hold her by the scruff of the neck, which only panicked her more. I was very glad to inch among the branches of the tree and hand the struggling bundle to Rouben.

Then a miracle happened. He clutched her tightly with his good left hand, but instead of ripping his flesh to shreds, the kitten became a purring bundle of soft fur at his touch. I watched the phenomenon with awe, and that, I suppose, is why I didn't hear anything from below until it was too late.

"Is Mrs. deMarchand or her daughter in?" a familiar voice asked, carrying above the closing of the small outer door. Then another voice, almost unfemininely low and dark, answered in chilling tones, "We are here, Mr. Eversleigh."

I gulped; it was not a good omen that my Aunt Felicité should sound so forbidding, but even had she been the sweetest person in the world, I should have been hard-put to explain my presence high in a tree in the middle of a bright sunshiny morning wearing nothing but the barest minimum of unmentionables, no matter how much they covered. It was not the most propitious of positions.

Had Mr. Eversleigh looked up, he would have had no difficulty spotting my white garments against the green of the tree or the red brick of the building; my only hope was to remain silent and still on my precarious perch until he should join them (*who?*) under the porchlike overhang. Then, with a bit of luck, I could clamber back onto the balcony and into my room without creating a fuss. It would have been nice to have a steadying hand from above, but Rouben had disappeared from the balcony the moment his kitten had been restored to him, apparently forgetting all else. Well, luckily I wasn't such a mewling miss that—

With an ominous creaking, punctuated by sharp retorts like derringer shots, the branch beneath me heaved and sank; it still clung to the tree, but it wouldn't for long with my weight resting on it. Now I would have to climb in earnest. I stretched out my arms toward the most likely handhold only to have it rise out of reach as my branch sank even lower.

"Good God!" Mr. Eversleigh roared.

"Mamma! Look!"

I had been discovered, yet somehow that seemed less important than avoiding an unpleasant fall to the flagstones below. It was not enough of a drop to kill me, but too much of one to escape unscathed. A large branch came within reach; though not thick enough to support me, it halted my inevitable slide downward, and, grabbing it, I hung suspended between the two branches like a treed coon.

"Is this my niece?" Aunt Felicité asked in frosty tones, then, without giving Mr. Eversleigh a chance to answer, went on, "I must admit I had no idea what sort of creature Pappa's mad idea might bring us, but I never dreamed to find her hanging naked in a tree!"

Apparently her opinion of me had been often expressed, for no one paid her venomous words any attention.

It was amazing how much I noticed while so dangerously suspended. Later I would have ample opportunity to study both Aunt Felicité and Cousin Charlotte, but there would be little I could add to my first impression.

Aunt Felicité was an imposing woman who had retained both her figure and her looks. In her youth she must have been a certified beauty; unfortunately, her temperament more nearly resembled that of the beast. Pride was writ large on that generous forehead, and selfishness pinched the corners of her lips. Her profile was naturally haughty and the lift of her chin turned it into arrogance.

By contrast, my first impression of Charlotte was one of softness and curves. She was pretty in a fluffy, nondescript sort of way, with gentle eyes and an unformed mouth. A person's mouth, Pa had maintained, was an indication of his character. By that yardstick, Aunt Felicité had too much and Cousin Charlotte none at all.

In coloring we were all surprisingly similar, with ample amounts of dark hair that sometimes had coppery highlights when exposed to bright light and creamy skin that became nut-brown at the first hint of sunshine. Mine already was; Charlotte's pale flesh had obviously been better protected.

Aunt Felicité pressed a lace-trimmed handkerchief against the general region of her heart and, with a touching sigh, slumped downward. I don't know if she expected Mr. Eversleigh to catch her or her daughter to help break her fall, but their eyes were riveted on me, and even I could hear her solid impact on the flagstones.

"Please ... help her," I cried, not then used to Aunt Felicité theatrics, but Mr. Eversleigh, his face grim with the effort of trying not to laugh, kept his eyes on me.

"You'd best be more concerned with yourself at the moment. Are you all right?"

There were several answers I could think of to that, but I knew he meant it kindly, so I merely responded, "Yes, for the moment. If I could just get up – "

"I think it would be best if you came down. Would you drop and trust me to catch you?"

"No," I answered without rancor. "I see no need to maim us both."

"Well, you certainly can't hang there all day." Laughter now colored his voice and his shoulders heaved slightly. I thought, uncharitably, that the wretch was enjoying my predicament.

"I have no such idea, sir," I said formally, beginning my descent. There was nothing to be gained in concealment now, so carefully I began to climb down, moving from one branch to another, testing each before entrusting my weight to it. That proved to be wise, for however sturdy the giant old tree seemed to be, I found it little more than a rotted hulk covered with the verdant guise of health.

Then, some ten feet above the ground, there were no more suitable footholds and I was forced to comply with

Mr. Eversleigh's suggestion. I lowered myself carefully until I was hanging only by my hands, which brought me within his reach. I didn't have to drop, merely release my grip and allow him to take my weight, but giving oneself and one's safety over into the hands of another is never a pleasant prospect.

Not that being folded into Mr. Jonathan Eversleigh's arms was unpleasant; quite the contrary. He cradled me like a babe, holding me close to his chest; he smelt of bay rum and new ironed linen and a certain indefinable scent that I identified just as man. I had never been held so before, at least not since my infant days, and surprisingly, it was most disturbing, opening doors and stirring cauldrons within my mind that I had never known existed. In that one moment the world changed irrevocably and not, I feared, for the better.

Chapter Five

It was with no little trepidation that I, now fully dressed and presentable, joined the others in the courtyard. Under the porchlike roof there was a very charming room, remarkable only in that it was outside the house and not in; later I would learn that most meals were served there during the hot weather, which was most of the time in New Orleans. There were chairs and couches and a table, all made of painted iron and covered with gaily printed cushions.

Everyone was seated at the table when I entered. They had not waited; an elderly Negro man was serving from a dented silver tray. Even he stopped dead to stare at me, and small wonder. Somehow Agnes had been there when I descended from the tree, ready to wrap me in a muffling robe, but the other servants had been just as fast; there had been a gallery of half a dozen black faces peering out from windows and doors as I had been quickly shuffled inside.

"Good morning," I said with a nonchalance I didn't feel. Pa had taught me well; sometimes a good bluff could be your best asset.

"Sit down, Genevieve," Aunt Felicité ordered in a voice that could freeze water. "I hope you have some explanation for your outrageous behavior."

I sat at my place, struggling to maintain a calm face. *Never let them see you're scared,* Pa had said; *never give them that power over you.*

Aunt Felicité passed me a cup of tea. The china was fragile and unbelievably thin, the tea fragrant with oranges and spice; I had never seen the like of either. The elderly manservant heaped my plate with enough food for several people, probably because he wanted to prolong his examination of this strange addition to the family; everyone else had normal portions in front of them.

Quite frankly, I was getting a little tired of being stared at; Aunt Felicité's glare was just this side of lethal, Jonathan Eversleigh's a queer mixture of apprehension and amusement; Cousin Charlotte watched me as one would an animal of uncertain domestication.

"Compassion, Aunt Felicité. I presume you are my aunt?" I added, trying to ignore how much my heart was pounding.

I thought Cousin Charlotte would faint. Apparently she had never seen her mother speechless before and did not know what to make of the situation. Unfortunately, Mr. Eversleigh not only approved but uttered a muffled snort of laughter, ill-disguised as a cough, which showed that he was actually enjoying the dowager's discomfiture.

"Compassion?" Her tone made it sound somehow suspect. "For whom? Certainly not for me!"

"It was not my intention to upset you, Aunt Felicité, and I do hope you are recovered from your fit of weakness … ? No, my compassion was for Uncle Rouben. At least, I assume it was my Uncle Rouben. I do not know who else it could have been."

My aunt made a choking sound, and, without intending to, I learned something; Aunt Felicité did not like her poor, disfigured husk of a brother—and that surprised me. I had been prepared for her dislike of me; after all, I was a stranger, an unknown quantity intruding into their well-ordered lives. But Rouben was her brother, her baby brother, and … I didn't understand.

"It was his kitten, you see. I was curious, so I opened the shutters for a glimpse of the house. Rouben was on the balcony. Poor thing, he was so distressed that his kitten had crawled out into the tree."

The story touched Cousin Charlotte; her pretty face shone with sympathy. "The poor thing. He loves that kitten; he loves all animals."

"Then he should have stayed at *Ombres*," Aunt Felicité said with asperity. "There are plenty of them there."

"Mamma, that's not fair," her daughter replied with more spirit than I would have thought she possessed. "You know Grandpappa wanted him to come see Dr. McCauley."

"We will discuss this later, Charlotte. There is no need to discuss family matters in front of strangers."

For a moment Jonathan Eversleigh's eyes held a twinkle, but then in the next breath they were remote and abstracted. "Oh, I don't think you need be so reticent, Mrs. deMarchand. Uncle Louis has often discussed Rouben's problems with me, and Genevieve is a member of the family."

Uncle Louis? That was something else Mr. Eversleigh had not mentioned, but there was no opportunity to pursue it further. Aunt Felicité began to speak, ostensibly to Charlotte, with the air of one taking a dose of nasty medicine.

"There is nothing Dr. McCauley or any other doctor can do. He has said so often. Pappa knows that."

"But perhaps Grandpappa feels he must keep trying, for his own sake as well as Uncle Rouben's," Charlotte said with surprising sympathy. For some reason I had not expected her to be so sensitive.

"Didn't you fear for your own safety?" Jonathan Eversleigh asked me directly. I could have slapped him for bringing up the subject of my behavior again when the memory of it appeared to be fading away. "That tree is rotten through; I've been telling Uncle Louis it should have been cut down years ago."

"The house was built around that old live oak," Aunt Felicité said indignantly, and again a spark of antagonism leaped between them. "It's the symbol of the house!"

"Then I hope the house is in better shape, for that old thing is a dangerous wreck." Mr. Eversleigh gestured languidly. He had pushed his scarcely touched plate aside and leaned back. Deep in his green eyes there was a sparkle, but I avoided his glance. Charming men were dangerous, especially when you found them attractive; charming men could ruin your life if you'd let them.

Hadn't my mother been proof of that?

Charlotte, at least, had the sympathy—or perhaps just the good manners—to see that I was uncomfortable; maybe she could picture herself in a similar situation, homeless and friendless in a strange place. Anyway, she smiled brightly at me and said, "What is your first impression of this part of the country, Cousin Genevieve?"

I returned her smile gratefully. It was a relief to be able to take refuge in casual conversation. "I am afraid I don't have much of one. It was quite late when we arrived last night and I was far too sleepy to see much beyond walls and streets. I am looking forward to learning about this area, though. There's only one thing..."

"What's that?"

"Is it always this hot?" I dabbed a handkerchief at the beads of perspiration on my upper lip.

"You'll find it gets worse before it gets better, Miss Bonneau," Jonathan Eversleigh said. He was smiling slightly, but I looked away without responding.

"Indeed," Charlotte said with a little laugh. "This is just spring! By the end of summer you'll know what hot is. Is that not so, Mamma?"

Aunt Felicité nodded abruptly. "Summers in New Orleans are always hot. That is why we are usually at *Ombres* by this time."

"I suppose the West is much different, Cousin Genevieve." Charlotte's voice was almost wistful.

I thought of tall pine-covered mountains and crisp streams and banks of sparkling snow, and my own voice became a little wistful. "Yes, very much."

"Did you have a summer place? Or is that not a custom in the West?" That was Aunt Felicité, and even though her tone was civil enough, I could not decide whether she was being snide or not.

"Summer places?" I thought of the open fields where we had camped, the leaky cabins, the occasional boardinghouse or hotel when Pa was in funds. "I suppose some people do. Pa and I moved around quite a bit."

"How exciting!" Charlotte cried, but any further questions she might have asked were cut short by the addition of another member to our party.

"And what do you find exciting, *ma chere* Charlotte?"

"Bastien!" Aunt Felicité purred with the first signs of real pleasure I had heard from her.

"Good morning, dear cousin," the newcomer said, bending elegantly over the mother's hand and then the daughter's. He seemed less happy to see Mr. Eversleigh, although his slight bow was very correct. "Eversleigh."

"Good morning, Thierry."

"I hadn't expected to see you here."

Aunt Felicité leaned forward and spoke with the air of one doing an unpleasant duty. "Genevieve, this is our cousin, Sebastien Thierry. Bastien, Genevieve Bonneau. Anton's child."

I had extended my hand straight out to be shaken in the western fashion; he took it gently between his soft fingers and, instead of shaking it, turned it until the back was uppermost, and there he planted just the barest hint of a kiss. "But of course. What have we been talking about for weeks but the advent of the mysterious lost cousin from the exciting West?"

Apparently he was no stranger to this household, for it took only a nod from Aunt Felicité for him to seat himself strategically between her and her daughter just as a cup of fragrant coffee appeared in front of him.

He was different from the dark southern French Bonneaus, this Sebastien Thierry. His classically chiseled face was pinkish, almost ruddy, and his sandy-red hair and grayish eyes as well as a slight but charming accent bespoke his northern French ancestry. Without exception, he was quite the handsomest young man I had ever seen, an impression only heightened by his gentle expression. But for all his good looks, he had an air of solid dependability. Perhaps this new life of mine was going to be better than I had thought.

"You called Aunt Felicité 'Cousin,'" I ventured shyly. "Does that mean you are a relation?"

The classic face broke into a merry grin. "Ah, *Mademoiselle* Genevieve, nothing would give me greater pleasure than to claim kinship with such a lovely creature as yourself, but I fear we share no common blood."

"I never heard that the Thierrys admitted to having anything common," Mr. Eversleigh said sardonically, lighting one of the thin cheroots he occasionally enjoyed.

"Your manners, sir, are only slightly worse than your breeding." Mr. Thierry's voice was still calm and urbane, but beneath the civilization was an edge.

"Bastien!" Aunt Felicité hissed, laying a hand delicately on his arm. "It is not worth it. Bastien is a relation of my late husband's family, Genevieve. His mother was Etienne's mother's cousin. On her mother's side," she added definitively.

Somehow that seemed dreadfully remote to me, too remote to bother much about, but Mother had talked of how back home relationships were valued and of how even the youngest children could know the exact relationship held with just about everyone they knew. I had always thought it something of a silly waste of time.

"And how are you, *ma chere* Charlotte?" Mr. Thierry asked, tenderly patting my cousin's arm. His gesture was proprietary, and I wondered if there was more than a remote cousinship between them. "I hope that the heat is not too much for you."

"No, it has been dreadfully exciting waiting for Cousin Genevieve to get here and going shopping. ... There are some lovely shops in New Orleans," she added to me. "I am so looking forward to showing them to you. Mamma wanted to do your shopping for you, but I felt sure you'd want to do it yourself."

Shopping? For what? I already had more clothes than I had ever owned in my life, but somehow I didn't think that was the thing to mention to Aunt Felicité.

"We were not sure of your coloration, my dear," the older woman said smoothly, "but as Bonneau blood tells, I predicted that you would take after your father ... as indeed you do. That will make things easier, for there are great amounts of suitable fabrics at *Ombres* the sewing women can make up without submitting you to the rigors of prolonged shopping after your long journey." Her smooth words flowed like cream, but I guessed that whatever she had told Charlotte she had never intended to take me around to the shops, where the rest of New Orleans might see what had invaded her family.

"Most considerate of you, I'm sure," Mr. Eversleigh said, and a slow smile indicated that he shared my opinion of my aunt's graciousness.

Sebastien Thierry gazed wiltingly at him for a moment. "It was most good of you to bring Mademoiselle Bonneau to us, *monsieur*."

Seemingly unwiltable, Jonathan Eversleigh puffed at his cheroot. "But since I've finished my errand, why don't I run along?"

"Of course I did not mean anything so crude. I merely thought that you are a very busy man and we have imposed too much on your time already."

"Same thing." He was imperturbable. "And I am busy, but Uncle Louis asked me to find his son and his granddaughter. I was too late to bring Anton back, but I did find Genevieve, and my duty will not be discharged until I deliver her safely into his hands."

"But surely that is ridiculous," Aunt Felicité said with a breathy little laugh. "You have fulfilled your duty and brought Genevieve as Pappa requested."

"But not to her grandfather."

"Your devotion is admirable, Mr. Eversleigh, but I assure you I shall take the utmost care of *Mademoiselle* Bonneau, just as I shall of *Madame* and *Mademoiselle* deMarchand."

Bastien's voice took on the slightest, most civilized edge.

"Most kind of you, Thierry, but unnecessary."

Aunt Felicité's tone became frosty. "Does this mean you intend to come with us to *Ombres*?"

"If you go in the next few days, yes. If you plan to stay on in town longer, I shall take her on to *Ombres* myself."

"Sir, I find your attitude insulting," Aunt Felicité bristled, but Jonathan Eversleigh seemed unfazed.

"I'm sorry if you do, but my plans are to follow through with my arrangement with Uncle Louis. If you care to come along, I would be delighted to have you."

"How dare you!" Aunt Felicité hissed, but Cousin Charlotte batted her eyes, asking, "Does this mean we will have the honor of your escort to *Ombres*, too, Mr. Eversleigh?" and I learned something else. My demure little Cousin Charlotte was absolutely fascinated by Mr. Jonathan Eversleigh!

* * * * *

We left for *Ombres* the next morning, and if I thought traveling with Mrs. Wooley had been a production, it was nothing compared to the state in which the deMarchands moved. First of all, there were three carriages; Aunt Felicité, Cousin Charlotte, and I rode in the first. I sat facing backward, as Aunt Felicité declared that neither she nor Charlotte could ride any way but facing forward without becoming deathly ill. It made no difference to me, but somehow I figured that their preference had more to do with status than with necessity.

Rouben and Agnes and the kitten rode in the second

carriage. At the last minute he had decided that he could not leave without the kitten, a fixture of the town house, and we were delayed some twenty minutes until it had been located, sound asleep on the drawing-room couch. Needless to say, Aunt Felicité did not find any of this fuss amusing.

Agnes was quite good with Rouben, coaxing him to obey, understanding his strange, garbled words and calming him when be became upset. When I offered to help, she made it very clear that he was her charge and no one else's. It was good that she was so attentive to him, for it seemed that no one else noticed him very much at all.

The third coach, carrying the servants and the luggage, was both larger and shabbier than either of the other two. It rode last in our little caravan, usually in the middle of the dust cloud kicked up by the other two vehicles.

Much to Aunt Felicité's visible disgust and Charlotte's barely-concealed pleasure, Jonathan Eversleigh did accompany us. He declined a grudgingly offered seat in the coach, preferring instead to ride alongside on a magnificent bay gelding. Every so often, obviously bored by the sedate pace of the carriage, he would leave the road and canter the bay out into some field. I watched enviously, the memory of my humiliating trip down the mountain on Jeb Hall's decrepit old mare still fresh in my mind. Very seldom had I known the privilege of riding a spectacular horse like the bay, but I remembered those times well, and somehow it made sitting in the poky old carriage that much more annoying.

Sebastien Thierry had brought his horse too, and one look was almost enough to make me forget the bay. Pale gold in color, with silver-gilt mane and tail, this silky creature was more beautiful than any I had ever seen. Mounted, Sebastien was quite as imposing as Jonathan and a great deal more elegant. His riding style was less robust than Jonathan's; later I would learn that he rode in the European style, where horse and rider become a fluid whole through a series of almost invisible commands. Next to him our rough-and-ready western way of riding seemed unbelievably crude. The contrast between the two men was fascinating, and I all but hung out the window watching.

We spent one night on the road, stopping at a small inn just at sundown. Aunt Felicité bore the ordeal with fortitude, insisting on seeing all the rooms in the inn only twice before choosing one that she thought might be suitable for the three of us. She then informed me that I was supposed to sleep with her and Charlotte, making it clear that the prospect was distasteful and undertaken only for my own protection. I remembered some of the places Pa and I had stayed and barely kept from laughing in her face.

I did laugh when the hotel servants came in and replaced the sheets with Aunt Felicité's own and, while doing so, made it clear they found her demands ridiculous. My aunt complained about their lack of sensitivity all evening. We retired early and my roommates fell into an exhausted sleep almost immediately; used to far more arduous journeys, I lay wakeful until long after moonrise, my eyes staring into the distance as if it were possible to pierce the dark and see the house named Shadows.

Chapter Six

S o you are the girl."

"I am Genevieve Bonneau."

A withered claw gestured toward a small chair directly under the nearest lamp. Despite the bright afternoon outside, the heavy velvet draperies were drawn, plunging the gloomy library into a stuffy dimness. Several lamps glowed in corners of the room, but their very brightness served to cloak the rest of the room in shadows that hid more than the light revealed. The heat made it all doubly oppressive.

"Genevieve Bonneau." His voice showed none of the age and weakness of his body as he mimicked my proud pronunciation. "You have your father's coloring. That answers one question, at least."

It took a moment for the enormity of his insult to my mother to sink in. When it did, I resisted my baser instincts for primitively physical action and stood with painful dignity. "I do not wish to continue this conversation," I said.

He drew in a sharp breath of surprise. I started toward the door, head held high, willing the tears not to appear in my eyes. I would not let this rude old man see my dreams die!

"Just where do you think you are going?" he snarled. I kept on walking, the unaccustomed bulk of skirts and petticoats making my step clumsy as I tried to avoid bumping blindly into the furniture. If I had been wearing my old pants and shirt, I should have been far beyond the reach of the shrunken figure in the rolling chair, but as it was, talonlike fingers closed on my skirt, effectively stopping me.

"Let go of me! I have no intention of staying where my mother's honor is insulted."

The thin mouth emitted a surprisingly robust laugh. "So you've inherited the Bonneau temper, too. I meant no insult to your mother, girl. Couldn't. Always tiresomely proper, as I remember. Now sit down."

"I prefer not to."

"I paid to find you, *mademoiselle*, and for your trip here and for all those pretty fripperies you're wearing, and I didn't do it just to have you walk away from me!"

I stared into blazing dark eyes, so like my own, and said as coldly as I could, "I was not aware that your generosity was intended as a business transaction, sir. I assure you your investment will be repaid. Kindly release me."

"Sit down, girl," he repeated in a much more reasonable tone. "So you got the Bonneau pride as well as the looks and temper. Damned uncomfortable package it is, too."

The papery old fingers released my skirt, but I couldn't make myself move. There was something in that voice, some note of wry regret that I had heard so often in Pa's voice, and it tugged at my heart. Perhaps I had been too hasty in judging this old man who was my father's father.

I had had no real expectations of what I should find at *Ombres*. Mother had talked about the place occasionally, but in all my memories I could not recall a straightforward description of it, so the low, rambling structure had been a pleasant surprise to me. There were two floors and enormous verandas in front on both, yet still the house appeared more modest in size than I had expected. Great live oak trees clustered protectively around the house, dwarfing it, their veilings of the fragile gray Spanish moss making it seem insubstantial and dreamlike.

It had been midafternoon when we arrived, and the low sun splashed everything with gold. Later I would see how dark the inside of the house was even on the brightest day, how the boards were warped and needing paint, but on that first afternoon it seemed aglow solely to welcome me home. Our arrival had been expected, for small Negro children had been set at the end of the drive to signal our approach, and in the hubbub of unloading I had barely been given time to freshen up before being summoned into my grandfather's presence.

Louis Philippe Montreaux Bonneau.

My grandfather.

His appearance had been a shock. I didn't know how a grandfather was supposed to look and I guess, despite Jonathan Eversleigh's dire counsel, I had built up a picture of a kindly old man with a twinkling eye and snowy beard who chuckled a great deal and spread favors around like sugar drops.

Even if I had listened to Mr. Eversleigh, I doubt I could have conjured up the illness-wasted body, permanently confined to a rolling chair, or the hawkish face—so close to what I remembered Pa's to have been before drink softened and blurred it—topped with a dark mane barely touched with gray. It took a second look to see the fragility beneath the face, the painful distortion of a once-powerful body, to see that this was just the husk of the man he had once been. Only his eyes gave an idea of times past; they were dark and strong and prideful, the eyes of a Bonneau.

I stared at him for a long moment, dark eyes locked with dark eyes in a look that was half battle and half unspoken communication. Then I sat down hesitantly, trying to make it seem an act of my own will and not a triumph of his.

I had not been pleased to notice when I'd entered the room that Jonathan Eversleigh was with my grandfather and apparently had been from the moment we had arrived. So he could hardly wait until we got there to report all my failings. Somehow I had expected better of him than that.

Both of them had looked sullen, and I had paused in the doorway, suddenly overwhelmed by the actuality of truly being there; entering that room was one of the most difficult things I had ever done. Jonathan Eversleigh had swept past me without a word, slamming the door behind him, and I was left alone with my grandfather.

Louis Philippe Montreaux Bonneau. My father's father. My grandfather and the coldest-eyed man I had ever seen. I had watched Pa in his prime dominate a poker table with sheer will. Now I saw where he had learned the trick. Those dark eyes could bore right through you.

"Good," my grandfather said, snapping me back to the present. "Now you just stay there. I didn't send Johnny all over hell and gone just to have you walk out on me in a huff."

"Why did you go to such lengths?" I asked coolly. "My father and mother left here years ago."

"Johnny said you were a sharp one. What answer did he give you to that question?"

"That you were fence-mending. Sort of."

He laughed again and still the sound seemed too vigorous, too powerful to have come from that wasted, dying body. "Sort of. Trust Johnny to protect himself. He should have been a lawyer, that one."

"Are you telling me that Mr. Eversleigh did not tell me the entire truth?" A funny feeling, the kind you get when you wake up to find a rattlesnake sharing your blanket, started to grow in my stomach.

"You ask penetrating questions, *Mademoiselle* Genevieve."

"And you seem quite good at avoiding them."

"*Touché*! A hit! I have never met a young woman with such an insistence on knowing the plain truth."

It struck me quite forcibly that he had called me a "young woman" instead of a "young lady." Mother had spoken often about the gulf between "woman" and "lady" and the great distinction between them though they both pertained to the same sex. I had no misconception about my dubious claims to ladyhood, but the denial of the title by a man who supposedly knew all the circumstances of my life stung. It gave a pretty good idea of what and how he thought of me and should have prepared me for what came later.

"However," he continued, his head nodding slowly, "I admire that. Not many people have the courage to ask for the truth, so I'll come right out with it. Johnny says you have no lawyer, no man of business."

A lawyer? For what? I picked up the silver thrown on the stage, took my pay from the saloon owner every Monday, paid the landlord, bought our meals, and tried to keep track of Pa's gaming debts. Sometimes they were high, but always more likely to be settled by guns or gold than by a man of business.

"No. I have never needed one. Pa..." I began and then quit, which was a mistake, for it made it seem I was making an emotional appeal. I had intended to say that Pa and I had not had enough money in recent years to worry about a man of business, but somehow, for Pa's sake, I didn't want to tell that to this hard-eyed old man. He probably knew already, from the invaluable Mr. Eversleigh, but he didn't have to know from me!

"I had hoped to handle this with your father."

Strange. He always said "him" or "your father," never "my son" or "Anton." That, too, should have prepared me.

"But as he is dead and you are here, I must deal directly with you. You are your father's only heir?"

"Yes. I was the only child that Mother and Pa had, and Pa never remarried after Mother died."

"No love children?"

If he had hoped to shock me, he failed. Anyone who has lived in a mining camp for long knows all about love children and a number of other things as well, including that a man whose world consisted of the poker table and a bottle had no interest in children, love or otherwise. I'm quite sure that had I been too young to do enough work to keep him comfortable, Pa would have abandoned me to the charity of Silver Bluff's citizenry long ago.

"None," I said coolly.

He looked at me speculatively but went on. "So you are the only one whom this would affect. I am an old man, *Mademoiselle* Genevieve, and it's time to set my house in order. There are certain things I want settled. I do not believe in leaving things to chance." He said the last few words as if they were a litany he had repeated often, but even that didn't warn me.

"Things?"

"*Ombres.* The land. Money. The things I leave behind. Look at all this! Do you think I inherited it like this?" he demanded, leaning forward in his chair until his face and burning eyes were just inches from mine. "No! My father was a gentleman who liked his leisure; he read his books, rode his horses, wrote his letters, and let his acres go to ruin! Then the War came and pretty damn near destroyed all that was left. It took me years of hard work to make *Ombres* into what you see today. I had to be cunning and ruthless and smart. You wonder why *Ombres* and the Bonneaus are doing so well when all our neighbors hardly have two coins to rub together?"

I must admit I had been curious. Even in the West we had heard of the terrible economic trials in the ruthlessly savaged South, and on the journey from New Orleans we had passed numerous residences all showing the devastating effects of unfamiliar poverty. To find *Ombres* comfortable and prosperous, much as it must have been before the War, had been both a pleasure and a puzzle.

He gave me no chance to answer; sitting back in his chair, he smote the arm sharply. "Because I was smart, that's why. Any of those fools could have seen that there was going to be a war and that the South would lose." There was something in his voice that sounded very much like sorrow. "No other way it could have ended. No heavy industry, no real army, nothing but pride and a belief in what was right – just like the men who fought against England that those Yankees are so damned proud of," he added bitterly.

Looking at this man who was my blood, my father's father, I felt a rush of pity. I sensed a feeling of regret, of a deep sadness that he knew himself unable to share fully the passions of his countrymen, even though their devotion had led to their ruin. Sometimes emotional detachment can be more painful than complete involvement.

Then he looked up again and the fierce gleam in those sunken old eyes burned away any such sentimental thoughts.

"I saw what was going to happen, saw it as early as 'fifty-eight. That's when I started sending gold to England. Real gold, not any of the worthless paper that's been floating around here for so many years. Couldn't touch it during the war, of course, but it was there when everything was over. It kept the land from going for taxes. Saved it all, I did, not like those damn fools who sacrificed everything for a lost cause—some of them right down to their wives' wedding rings. I've fought hard for what I've built, and I don't intend to see it challenged or torn apart after I'm gone." He reached over to the velvet-shrouded table for a single sheet of paper, which he tossed almost contemptuously in my lap. "Sign that."

I unfolded it gingerly, aware even then that I didn't want to know what it contained. "And this is why you brought me here?"

"Yes. There are pen and ink beside you."

It wasn't very long, just a couple of paragraphs, lines on a paper that gave the final blow to the rosy dream I had been building, in spite of all common sense, ever since Jonathan Eversleigh had appeared in my cabin that night more than two weeks before.

I read the terse words once, then once again, and lowered the paper with shaking hands.

"Well? Do you understand what that means?" he asked impatiently.

"My mother saw to it that I had more than sufficient education, Mr. Bonneau. This means you want me to sign away any claim I or my heirs might have against you, your estate, or your other heirs. You sought me out and brought me halfway across the continent just to sign this?"

"I had originally planned to talk with your father...,"he began, then took one look at my furious face and stopped.

"And you would have done this to him? Your own son?"

"He chose to leave this house, to abandon this land. He has no right to any of it."

"Mr. Bonneau," I said in an ice-cold voice, "until your agent found me, I had no knowledge of you or what you had or this place. What makes you think—"

"Greed! Sooner or later you would have remembered, or someone would have remembered for you. Nobody ever really forgets money. Felicité stayed here. She looks after her poor brother. Everything should go to her line...to Charlotte." He pounded the arm of his rolling chair as if I could have possibly missed the point, but I was more interested in the way he had said "her poor brother," not "my poor son." Apparently Louis Philippe Montreaux Bonneau acknowledged as his kin only those who pleased him.

"That is logical."

"Did you read all of that? Understand it?"

"Quite well."

"Then you see I'm not sending you away empty-handed. I was prepared to settle a fair amount on your father."

"Buy him off, you mean." The words were out before

I could stop them, but to tell the truth, I would have made little effort to do so.

"If you must be vulgar. I'll settle the same amount on you. From what Johnny says you can certainly use it, and you'll probably make better use of it than your father ever would."

"Now you are vulgar, as well as rude." To say nothing of Mr. Jonathan Eversleigh! I could think of quite a few things I wanted to say to him as well, none of them very nice. My grandfather's age might protect him from the brunt of my wrath, but Mr. Eversleigh had no such protective venerability.

"You will watch your tongue, miss!"

"No, you will watch yours!" I stood and slowly began to shred that damnable paper into tiny, tiny pieces. "How dare you bring me here, dangle the prospect of a family and a welcome in front of me, and then throw this ... this insult in my face!"

His eyes narrowed to dangerously flashing slits. "Stop that! I never intended—"

"I don't care what you intended. I never would have thought of putting any claim against any part of this, and I never will. How dare you insult your own blood like this!"

"No one was ever insulted by money."

"I am. Like this I am."

"You're quite cavalier about money for someone who doesn't have any. Did you see how much I am prepared to give you?"

"I have excellent eyesight," I snapped, tearing even

more furiously at the hateful scraps of paper.

"Don't think you'll hold me up for more. That's the only offer you'll get!"

"I don't want any offer. I don't want anything you have to offer! I am accustomed to earning my own way." I was losing my temper and that was bad; Pa always said that when you lost your temper, you lost control of the situation. Unfortunately, I always remembered that too late.

"As a saloon singer!"

"As a saloon singer, but at least my money is my own and not a handout from a bad-tempered old man!" I stopped, teeth sunk into my underlip, and took a deep breath. Had I been in less of a state, I might have worried about the old man. He looked as if my words had been blows.

When I spoke again, I was in control once more. My words were clipped and businesslike. "It will take a while, but you have my word ... the word of a Bonneau," I added ironically, "that you will be repaid every cent for my trip here and for the clothes you ordered purchased for me and for any other expenses that might have been incurred on my behalf. I have no desire to be indebted to you." In an extravagant gesture, I flung the scraps of paper to the floor. "I wish nothing from you."

Louis Philippe Montreaux Bonneau was indeed used to having his own way. Probably no one except the invading Yankees had ever challenged his wishes since my father had run away a generation ago, and his anger was obvious. "Listen to me–!"

"No, I will not. If it weren't so late, I would leave right this very minute. Don't forget to include the charge for tonight's lodging in the tally of what I owe!"

"Come back here!" he roared as I swept from the room, this time too quickly to be held back, skirts or no skirts. He kept on shouting even after I had childishly slammed the door behind me.

Without question, the great Louis Philippe Montreaux Bonneau was used to getting his way, but he had forgotten that I, too, was a Bonneau!

Chapter Seven

When I reached the lovely, airy room that had been allotted to me, I was still shaking, though I couldn't tell if it was from anger or fear.

When Aunt Felicité had first told me this room was to be mine for the length of my visit, I had been enchanted. Great open windows looked out over rolling green fields to tropical-looking woods; crisp thin white curtains fluttered in the breeze that had not yet begun to cool off for evening. The room was yellow and white, with a dark wooden floor punctuated by colorful islands of rag rugs. The furniture was simple, probably made by the slaves right here when the house had been built. It was a room where I had felt, however foolishly, that I might be at home.

Never grab the pot until you know what the other fellow's cards are, Pa had said. I had always thought Pa picked up his knowledge about cards and people during his years as a professional gambler; now I was beginning to wonder if he learned the basics of survival within his own family.

Deft hands had been at work during my absence. As if by magic, my cases had been unpacked and all my possessions put away in the big walnut chest of drawers and the even bigger armoire. Although I now possessed more than I ever had in my life, my wardrobe looked pathetically skimpy and forlorn in those enormous pieces of furniture.

I yanked viciously at the bell pull. A quick search of the room had revealed nothing of my cases; in a house this grand they probably had a special room just for luggage. Well, they could just bring mine back, because I was going to be gone the first thing in the morning! In fact, if the sun had not already been flirting with the western horizon—or if I had been more familiar with the territory—I should have started out then and there.

"Well? What happened?"

Charlotte stood in the door, her face alive with curiosity. Such animation made her seem very pretty. I stared blankly at her, wondering how it would be to lead her life, and I confess I envied her. She had always had a family; known where her next meal was coming from, who her people were, and where she belonged – where she always had and always would belong, without question. I felt a thousand years older than she could ever be.

"Genevieve! You look so strange. What happened? Are you all right?"

I blinked away surprising tears of self-pity and shame, and looked away as she grabbed my arm in her distress. At least there was one Bonneau with true charity in her heart toward me.

"I'm fine, thank you."

"Poor darling! I know Grandpappa can be a bit overwhelming at times, but you'll get used to him." She chattered on, unaware that her blithe assumption that I would stay was like salt in a deep cut.

"Yes, *mademoiselle*?" Agnes had entered the room silently and stood in front of the tiny fireplace like some sort of carved heathen idol.

"Oh, Agnes, do go away!" snapped Charlotte pettishly, but—once more in control of myself—I motioned her to hush and stepped forward.

"Please, Charlotte, I rang for her. Agnes, where are my cases?"

If she was surprised, no emotion passed the rigid barriers of her face or voice. "Your luggage was taken to the attic as soon as it was unpacked, mademoiselle. Is something missing?"

"Nothing is missing. I would like it brought back down as quickly as possible."

"Tonight, mademoiselle?" Agnes asked and, at my definite affirmative, nodded her head and left as quietly as she had come.

Charlotte was looking at me as if I had lost my mind. "Your luggage, Genevieve? Why on earth do you want your luggage tonight?"

"I am leaving in the morning, Charlotte. I should like to get my packing done tonight."

The soft mouth fell open in surprise. "Leaving? Genevieve, what happened? Grandpappa—"

I should have kept my mouth shut. This innocent babe couldn't even begin to understand my feelings, but I could not hold the words back. "Your Grandpappa is a horrible, vicious, dreadful old man!" I snapped with more venom than intended. At this moment it was either anger or tears, and at least anger was sometimes a constructive emotion.

"You look fit to do murder! What on earth did Grandpappa say to you?"

"I think the question is more what Genevieve said to Pappa!" exclaimed Aunt Felicité as she strode into the room, her Bonneau eyes snapping with Bonneau temper. Did no one in this household ever knock? "You can hear him yelling all over the ground floor. Really, Genevieve, you should have remembered that he is an old man in poor health. What can you have been thinking of to upset him so?"

So I was guilty without even the courtesy of a hearing. That seemed typical. It was beyond her comprehension that he might have upset me—though, to be fair, her loyalty should be to her father.

It was a familiar feeling, though; whatever the Bonneaus wanted to believe automatically became unassailable truth. Pa had been good at that and had been angered when fortune or the rest of the world didn't bow automatically to his desire of the minute.

"I am sure you will calm him down, Aunt Felicité."

"But Genevieve," Charlotte interrupted, "what is this all about? Why are you leaving? Where will you go?"

Aunt Felicité suddenly looked like a cat who had found an unguarded milk pail, though she struggled to keep her features calm. "Leaving?"

"Yes. I think all of us will be happier if I do," I said coolly. "I intend to leave first thing in the morning."

"Mamma!" cried my cousin in real distress. "Tell her she can't—"

"Hush, Charlotte." Aunt Felicité inclined her head regally, an insufferably smug smile on her lips. "We mustn't stand in Genevieve's way if this is what she really wants."

Either she wasn't aware of the offer her father had made me or didn't know I had refused to sign; otherwise she would not have been taking my imminent departure so complacently. I tended to believe she didn't know about that iniquitous paper at all, for if she did, Aunt Felicité would never have let me leave with it unsigned. She would have understood no better than her father why I would not sign that horrible document, or that I would never think of laying claim to any part of the estate.

"It is," I replied firmly to Aunt Felicité's statement.

"But you can't!" Charlotte wailed. "Genevieve, we've just found you."

"Charlotte, that will be enough. I'm sure Genevieve is quite capable of making her own decisions."

Then my cuddly little kitten of a cousin turned into a hissing cat. Linking her arm through mine, she turned to face her mother's freezing stare, which was an act of no small courage. "You say I am not capable of making decisions, but we are much of an age."

"That is true, but Genevieve has had a vastly different life than you, my child."

It was true, but she didn't have to make it sound so

deadly an insult.

"Come, Charlotte," my aunt said in a tone that was both civil and impossible to disobey. "We must not keep Genevieve from her packing."

Her surprising moment of challenge over, Charlotte threw me a sympathetic look and a wan smile as the door closed behind them.

At least I would have the memory of one friend among my father's family, I thought later; that and memories of *Ombres*. It was nearly dark now. The sky overhead went from a glowing orange in the west to a brilliant purple directly above me to a thick night-blue in the east. It hadn't been spectacular like our gaudy mountain sunsets, but there had been a coziness, a delicacy about the dying day that seemed entirely in keeping with the gentle land.

After Aunt Felicité and Cousin Charlotte had left my room, I felt too restless to stay indoors. I decided to explore the outside of *Ombres*, storing up memories of the sights and sounds and smells of this unknown ancestral home. I should have liked to do the same inside, seeing the rooms where my father grew up, but there were too many people in there, too many people I didn't want to see, so I contented myself with the outside.

I walked the ragged paths of the ruined garden against whose roses my mother had always compared all others, saw the tumbled pile of gray latticework that must have once been a gazebo, walked past a row of neatly whitewashed little houses that had once been

called slave quarters and were now called just the
quarters. They still housed the same people doing the
same jobs on the same land; now, however, that land was
drenched in uselessly shed blood.

I peeked into the enormous stable, which was finer
than most of the places that had ever sheltered me, and
touched curious, velvety noses. I found the struggling
remnants of an orchard and the dark shade of a vigorous
scuppernong arbor. To the east of the house I could hear
the merry melody of a running creek, softer and slower
than our mountain ones, as if it, too, were bound by the
lazy spell of this land, but the underbrush was too thick
to penetrate without serious damage to my skirts, and
there was not enough light to seek a path.

At last I found an old swing hung from an ancient
live oak and merely sat there, watching the sun die
through a shredded gauze veil of Spanish moss and
listening to the night sounds grow.

It seemed so strange to me that this had been Pa's
home, and that he had so seldom mentioned it;
tomorrow had always mattered more to him than today
or yesterday. It had been Mother who longed for *Ombres*
and for all it represented. In turn, she spoke very little of
the rooms above the store, where she had been raised
among her brother and sister-in-law's brood, half as
helper, half as child. My questioning of the reluctant Mr.
Eversleigh had produced no recognition of the names of
any of Mother's family in the area since the War. Had
any of them still been in Furneaux, I should have
appealed to them for lodging, despite Mother's dire tales

of their tight-lipped Puritanism. But it was just as well; I had looked after myself and Pa, too. Looking after just me couldn't be any worse.

"Such a sad face, *Mademoiselle* Bonneau. Perhaps you regret your hasty decision to leave?"

Aunt Felicité had certainly wasted no time in spreading the joyous news, I thought, and in doing so did her a disservice, for it had been Charlotte who told him and appealed for his aid. In the semidarkness Mr. Thierry was very handsome, even more so than in the daylight, and that took some doing.

"No. It is for the best."

With a graceful motion, he seated himself on the narrow swing, waiting only a moment for my nod of permission. "For the best of whom? Surely not for me."

"You?"

"Certainly me. If you go, I shall have to follow, as I cannot allow such beauty and grace to pass from my life." Somehow he had gotten possession of my hand and was gently teasing the back of it with his lips. Even in the thickening dark I could see the light in his eyes. "You could not expect to come into my life and then think I would let you leave it so soon."

In spite of myself, my heart and stomach gave convulsive little flip-flops. That I knew exactly what he was doing did not lessen its initial impact.

Most people think of the West as a wilderness full of rough-and-ready semi-savages; a great deal of it is like that, of course, but people of all types drift through, people like Mother and Pa, who knew more than just mountains and prairies and survival. For example, there was the Count; if he had another name, I never heard it, but when he was in his cups—which was most of the time—he talked of France and of his family's estates, and some of us believed his title was genuine. Anyway, the Count felt it a point of duty to flirt with every female within range; luckily, by the time I got big enough to attract his interest, I had seen him in action enough to realize that all his pretty words and high flattery might make a girl feel wonderful but never seemed to do her any good. Sebastien Thierry was younger, better-looking, and cleaner than the Count had ever been, but he sounded just like him.

"I cannot see where I affect your life at all, Mr. Thierry," I said coolly, and reclaimed my hand.

"Ah, cruel beauty! You will break my heart—"

"Piffle! Use your pretty speeches on my cousin Charlotte. I feel she will appreciate them more than I."

He sighed and placed a limp hand over the region of his heart. "Alas, she is as hard-hearted as you. I am doomed to die of unrequited..."

He was still talking, but enough was enough, especially on an empty stomach. Besides, it was full dark by now, and if sitting outside alone in the night with a man was considered questionable behavior in Colorado, I could just imagine how it would be looked upon in Louisiana!

"That's all very nice, Mr. Thierry, but it is getting late and—"

He slapped his forehead in a theatrical gesture. "And

is that not proof of what I have just been saying? I came to tell you that dinner will be served shortly, and the sight of your beauty and the thought of an opportunity to have a little private conversation—"

"Are you trying to tell me supper's ready?" I stood and put anxious hands to my disheveled hair.

It looked worse than it felt. After a hasty escape to my room, I examined the damage and groaned. Smudges adorned my face, complementing the leaves that nestled shyly in my hair, and as for my dress ... nothing less than a complete laundering could ever make it presentable again. Maybe I could just have something brought to my room? It was a cowardly thought and I squelched it ruthlessly.

"*Mademoiselle* has been taking a walk?"

I looked up further in the mirror saw the reflection of Agnes standing impassively by the fireplace. Why in the world did anyone bother with doors in Louisiana, since no one seemed to pay any attention to them?

"What are you doing in here?"

"Why, waiting for you, mademoiselle, to help you dress."

Now, I had been dressing myself for a great number of years, but I had also learned that what were simple words in Colorado had a variety of meanings down here.

"Dress?"

"To change into your pretty frock. Since you were so late, I took the liberty of choosing an outfit for you."

She certainly had. Across the bed lay the most elaborate dress I owned. In Denver Mr. Eversleigh had insisted that I have a dress for evening, and, putting their heads together, the gaggle of seamstresses had come up with a creation that I was convinced was far too grand for me ever to use. Of dull gold taffeta, it was cut lower in front than any costume I had ever dared to wear while singing. It fit like another skin down to my waist all around and almost that tightly in front clear down to the floor, all the skirt material being pulled into a great knot and spill in the back. The sleeves were mere narrow bands of silky dark gold fringe around the top part of my arms. There was more fringe hung here and there on that mass of material in the back; it looked almost as if someone's parlor curtains had fallen on me.

"Just for supper?"

A strange look fluttered over Agnes's frozen features. "As you know, mademoiselle, your lady aunt requested a special dinner for this evening, and that means changing. Now there is no time to send for a bath, so if mademoiselle will wash her face and arms quickly, I will see what can be done to her hair."

Well, I knew nothing of the sort, but it seemed in keeping. A special dinner, everyone nicely dressed, and I come trotting down in a day dress. I would have made Aunt Félicité ecstatic if I had had leaves in my hair!

Of course, I realized that Agnes might have been manipulating me for her own reasons, but I didn't believe it a minute. By telling me a direct lie, she would be leaving herself wide open for retribution. No, for some reason she had decided to ally herself with me, for this evening at least, and was telling me what I should know in the only way a servant could ... and I was very grateful.

It took some doing, but by the time the dinner gong sounded, I looked a different person. Cleaned of all evidences of the outdoors, poured and pinched and pushed into that golden monument of a dress, I was sitting quite still—as if that bodice would permit anything else—while Agnes worked magic with my hair. There had not been time, she apologized, for anything fancy, but obviously her idea of fancy was quite different from mine, for where I would have settled for a neat chignon, she swept my thick dark mass of hair upward, pinning here, curling there, tucking and pulling and tweaking until I was fidgeting.

The gong had sounded twice now, and she was rolling up the same curl and pinning it in exactly the same place for the third time.

"Agnes?"

"My apologies, *mademoiselle*. I did not mean to make you late," she said with smooth contradiction, and once more I realized how stupid I was. Again, she couldn't say anything, couldn't cross or badmouth her employers, but for whatever reason of her own, she wanted me to make an entrance and this was her way of assuring it.

"Think nothing of it."

"*Mademoiselle* looks very pretty tonight."

"Thank you," I said automatically before glancing in the long mirror and really seeing myself for the first time.

It was silly, but when I looked in the pier glass across

the room, I wondered who had come into my room without knocking this time. Was that really I, that elegant vision in dull gold? Already my shamefully brown skin was fading into a ripe tawny color that complemented the gold of the gown and made the cluster of dark curls draped with casual artifice over my bare shoulder that much more dramatic. For the first time in my life I wished for jewelry. My ears and bosom and arms seemed too exposed, too bare.

Well, there was nothing that could be done about that, so I lifted my head proudly and turned to Agnes with speaking eyes. "Thank you," I said again, and she nodded with proper humility, but her lips curved upward in a little smile as she seemed to understand my thoughts.

I took one last look in the mirror, pirouetting so that the fringe stood out, before stepping into the hall. Let the Bonneaus do their worst! I was ready for them.

Chapter Eight

G ood God!" he gasped, and, thinking I was alone in the shadowy hallway, I jumped.

I had been prepared for just about anything from the Bonneaus— hatred, sarcasm, coldness—but Jonathan Eversleigh was not a Bonneau, and his look of surprise (which was rapidly changing to one of narrow-eyed speculation) was unnerving. Since it was so late, I had expected to be the last one upstairs. As soon as I could get enough breath inside that tight golden bodice, I told him so.

He walked around me slowly, as men buying livestock will around a likely-looking beast, his eyes aglow with a queer blend of admiration and sarcastic amusement. In that instant the glory of my beautiful dress faded and I was once more the half-wild saloon singer of Three Mile Creek as surely as if I wore Pa's ragged old shirt and pants beneath the luxurious taffeta. He would always see me in them, no matter what I wore, I thought, and his next words confirmed it.

"I came to see if you were dressed," he said enigmatically. "Is this one of the things from Denver?"

"Don't you know? You paid for it."

"Your grandfather paid for it, and it appears to have

been one of the best investments he ever made. I merely handed over the money."

He made another circuit of me, and this time I had the odd feeling that my dress had ceased to exist, that I was naked to my very soul. It was a look that saloon singers became used to, one that clearly defined their status as objects of some sort of entertainment or another, and I had always resented it very much; the most disturbing thing about it now was that it didn't disturb me much at all.

This was the first time I had seen him in evening clothes. The dazzlingly white shirt, ornamented with severe little ruffles and dark opaque studs that absorbed the light, set against the stark black suit, looked very well on his rangy height; in fact, he was most devastatingly handsome, but I had acknowledged that for some time. The low lamplight glinted off his hair, making it appear almost the same shade as my gown.

"A pity you handed over so much," I said at last, erroneously blaming my breathlessness on the gown's tight bodice. "It will take me that much longer to repay."

One eyebrow lifted slightly. "I heard about your meeting this afternoon. Are you really leaving in the morning?"

"As soon as I can finish packing and be gone."

"Going down with all flags flying," he said with more than a little sarcasm, gesturing to my gown. "Or is this merely a diversionary action, to make your grandfather … or perhaps the attentive Monsieur Thierry …regret your leaving enough to beg you to stay?"

My hands clenched into fists, the nails making painful little half moons into my flesh. "That's fine talk from someone who brought me halfway across the continent into this damned mess and didn't even have the decency to tell me what to expect. I hope you enjoyed the show, Mr. Eversleigh!" I hissed, tightening my fists until the knuckles were dead white. It was that or fly clawing at his face.

"You little witch," he growled, "I should beat the tar out of you for that! For your information, I didn't know what he was up to until this afternoon, and I told him that if I had known what he was planning I wouldn't have gone in the first place!"

"You did?" Somewhere down deep inside me something leaped with pleasure, but I stomped it down ruthlessly. Words are easy enough to say after the deed has been done and easier to believe if one really wants to. That doesn't make any of it true. "I wish you had known!"

"I saw how sad you were I interrupted your little tryst with that gorilla in your cabin! Perhaps I should have saved myself the trouble of interfering!"

Curse the man! How *dare* he? I did lose control then, taking a wild swing, which he ducked easily, imprisoning my right hand in his. I tried to tell myself that were I less restrictively clad I would have jumped him, flailing with foot and claw, but even if the golden dress had permitted violent movement, I had somehow passed beyond such primitive action. Perhaps it was the atmosphere of *Ombres* or perhaps I had myself changed in some way—or perhaps I was just smart enough not to start something I had no hope of winning.

That did not mean I went happily into defeat. I twisted and pulled, trying to free my hand—and why were these Southern men so obsessed with hands? Sebastien Thierry was always kissing them, and now Jonathan Eversleigh seemed to have taken permanent possession of mine. There was no pain in his grip as long as I did not resist; when I struggled, I could feel my bones bend. What was really insulting was that he made it look so effortless.

Never releasing my hand, he threaded it through his left arm and held it against muscle scarcely more yielding than stone, all in a fair counterfeit of solicitude. "Don't struggle so! You are only going in to dinner, not to your execution."

"Let go of me!"

"Why? It is considered polite for a lady in formal dress to be escorted in to dinner by a gentleman."

"I didn't choose this abominable dress," I growled through grinding teeth. "Agnes did."

It sounded like he muttered, "So she didn't tell you," but then he chuckled, an unholy smile lighting his face, and I thought I must have misunderstood, for in the next instant he was quite serious. "And you really intend leaving in the morning?"

"I do," I replied with proud hauteur. "I suppose transportation can be arranged for me to the nearest town?"

"I suppose. What will you do when you get there?"

"What anyone would do . . . try to find work."

"As a singer?"

"Still afraid that I shall prove an embarrassment to the Bonneaus? Don't worry; I have no desire to stay in this region any longer than I have to."

"Miss Bonneau, I know you are a brave and resourceful young lady, but you must be reasonable. How will you live?"

"I will manage."

"By begging in the streets? Or perhaps by slipping into an even less pleasant trade?"

Then I struggled in earnest for my freedom, wanting nothing more to than to scratch out those probing green eyes. "You dare!" I lashed out with my foot and felt it make definite contact with his shin, but other than a slight twitch of his lips, he gave no sign that I had touched him.

"I just want to make you think," he said, his hand firm against mine. "How will you survive until you find work, if you do find work?"

"I can look after myself," I spat. "I've got money!"

"Money?"

"Yes! Almost fifty dollars, so I don't have to crawl to anybody for anything!"

Again my quick tongue had betrayed me. That almost fifty dollars was my secret, had been my secret for years, ever since I had started saving it a penny and a nickel at a time, when I had first seen how perilous living with Pa could be. Sometimes when he was too drunk to know how much he had won, I would filch a little and stash it away. Pa never knew of its existence, but it fed us more than once during the worst times. Of course, in the early days it hadn't been anywhere near fifty dollars and things had to be really desperate before I would touch it. After I started singing and money was not such a day-to-day problem, I added more and more to my little hoard and touched it less and less, knowing that in Mother's old worn coin purse, usually tucked somewhere on my person during the day or placed under my pillow at night, that almost fifty dollars was my protection and my independence.

For a moment I was afraid that he might laugh, but he didn't. The generous lips twitched and then thinned. "Fifty dollars. Almost fifty dollars. That wouldn't last very long, you know."

"Not for you," I said spitefully and in ignorance. "It would do me quite a while."

"Yes, Gene Bonner, I bet it would, but it doesn't have to. Why don't you stay here?"

For a minute I had almost let myself like him. I hadn't been called Gene Bonner since Wally Hauptmann had shouted a farewell to me as we rode down the mountain from Three Mile Creek. I should have remembered Eversleigh was my grandfather's hireling.

"Would you take that old man's filthy deal?" I asked.

"No, and if I were younger, I'd probably stalk out in a temper just like you're doing, but that doesn't make it the smartest thing to do. I'm not asking you to stay forever, Miss Bonneau, and I'm not saying you should sign that agreement if you don't want to. What I am saying is that I think you should stay here for a few days; see the place, get to know your people, have a bit of respite from having to fend for yourself."

He spoke so earnestly that I could not help but be touched. No one had spoken to me so since Mother's death, and even if it were a lie, I allowed myself the comfort of it for just a minute.

"It can be quite pleasant here," he went on, his hand on mine now more protecting than imprisoning. "You get to know *Ombres* and I'll see what I can do about making Uncle Louis see things a little more reasonably."

A lifetime of lessons is not easily unlearned. I looked up quickly. "And what's in it for you?"

For a moment his eyes blazed. "You are the damnedest, most suspicious – I'll tell you what's in it for me! Just so I'll know that once someone did something for you simply for the devilment of it and that you'll probably spend the rest of your life wondering what I got out of it!"

"And are you used to having people do things for you for nothing?"

"You are a witch, Gene Bonner, or Genevieve Bonneau, or whoever you are," he said at last and without heat. "I should just throw you in and let you fend for yourself, but I could never resist a drowning kitten. Let's simply say I have my own reasons and leave it at that. A few days here won't hurt you, and if things become too uncomfortable or just don't work out, I'll see you get back to Colorado myself."

Already I was thinking that a few days couldn't make

any difference, that the world would still be there whenever I wanted to return to it. As long as my almost fifty dollars was safe and I was well enough to walk, I had nothing to fear.

Green eyes looked down at me. "Deal?"

"What about my gran– old Mr. Bonneau? He may not want me staying here."

"He won't object," Jonathan Eversleigh said with finality. "Deal?"

"Deal."

He drew a deep breath. "At last! I hope you never take up horsetrading, young lady. You'd have the entire state in chaos within a week." He smiled as he said it, though, and then that unholy amusement glittered in his eyes again. "Shall we go down to dinner? We don't want to keep your aunt waiting any longer."

Chapter Nine

If I needed any proof that Aunt Felicité had meant to embarrass me, it was writ plain on her face as Mr. Eversleigh and I paused on the landing. Both she and Charlotte had changed into evening dresses, and while neither was as spectacular as mine, both Aunt Felicité's garnet-colored silk and Charlotte's simpler but stunning figured muslin would have made my day dress look like a street urchin's costume, even if it had been clean.

The staircase came down in two flights, and one could not be seen by anyone in the hallway or in the drawing room just beyond until one reached the landing. With the instincts of a showman, Mr. Eversleigh stopped on the landing, giving everyone a good look at us, his unrelenting grip on my hand as good as a rein.

"It is not *Mademoiselle* Bonneau," Sebastien Thierry breathed. "It is a goddess!"

"Cousin Genevieve, how wonderful you look! Where did you get that dress?" cried Charlotte even as her mother, adeptly recovering her composure, spoke with kindly condescension, "Indeed, but perhaps a trifle grand for a simple family dinner?"

However reluctantly, I had to admire her coolness. If I had come down in my day dress, stained or unstained, she doubtless would have made some remark about western barbarians who do not dress for dinner. It would have been interesting to see how she handled herself in a poker game.

"Ah, but this is not just a simple family dinner, my dear Mrs. deMarchand," Mr. Eversleigh said with a tiny, uncomfortable smile. "It is a celebration."

"A celebration?" Mr. Thierry asked, but Charlotte seemed to catch on right away. Her face lit up with a gay smile. "You've decided to stay, that's it, isn't it?"

It warmed my heart to see how pleased she was. I nodded. "For a few days."

"Indeed," Aunt Felicité said frostily, and it was the last thing she said until we were well into dinner. Not that anyone seemed to notice, for the air was filled with Charlotte's happy babble of what we must do and the places we must see and the people I must meet. Even if we did only a few of the things she listed, I should be there for weeks, and though I had no intention of that, her chatter was far preferable to the heavy atmosphere it veiled.

The dining room was enormous, taking up almost one side of the house. There was the constant dark wood floor, bare of any rugs, a table as long as the bar in Three Mile Creek, and a sideboard covered with serving dishes and utensils. One wall was solid French doors, all thrown open to catch any coolness the night might offer. Over the table hung a great square silk fan, embroidered with flowers, and powered by a small boy in the corner tugging on a cord; the fan swept lazily back and forth over our heads, disturbing the insects almost as much as it did the candle flames that attracted them. The table was covered in blindingly white linen, flowered china that all matched, and half a mountain's worth of silver.

A simple family dinner, indeed!

We seated ourselves, the others apparently according to established custom, I where Mr. Eversleigh left me before he went to fetch my grandfather. Two servants moved with silent grace, filling water and wine glasses on the table and carrying things back and forth from the sideboard.

I stared at my place in dismay. Two plates, four glasses, over a dozen pieces of silverware ... It was overwhelming, and yet –

The entrance of my grandfather commanded all eyes as Mr. Eversleigh pushed in his rolling chair. He, too, wore evening dress, and in the flattering light one could almost forget that he was an old and sick man. He looked up to murmur something to Mr. Eversleigh, and although I had not noticed a resemblance between them before, in that instant it was pronounced, raising a quick, ugly question in my mind.

Why did Jonathan Eversleigh want me to stay?

"Yes, Uncle Louis, I have persuaded little Genevieve not to go for a few days."

Dark eyes swept over me, and although their expression did not change, I sensed both admiration and satisfaction. "Is that true, girl?"

I smiled as regally as I could. "Only for a few days. It seems a shame to come this far and not see the country. A short visit will make no difference to my original plan."

The old man must have been expecting my complete capitulation, for that didn't please him. He frowned and said something about being tired of having to wait for his dinner. Aunt Felicité made an imperious gesture and the meal began.

It was the moment I had dreaded. I stared down at my place as a bowl of clear soup was put in my plate. There were only three spoons and – of course! I drew a breath of relief. No wonder there had been that air of familiarity. I had seen all this before; not, of course, in glittering silver and flowered china in a gracious dining room. It had been in the back of Bonneau's Restaurant in Silver Bluff, and there had been chipped thick crockery and little bits of wood, which my mother had labeled *oyster fork* and *butter knife*.

I think Aunt Felicité was disappointed when the display of cutlery didn't upset me. Charlotte and Sebastien Thierry seemed to accept my prowess as normal, but there was a look of curiosity in Jonathan Eversleigh's eyes. My grandfather kept his head down, concentrating on his food, and everyone was very careful not to notice how his hands shook.

The soup was replaced by delicate fish, which was in turn followed by a grayish meat served with mint sauce. It was quite good, and from the unending stream of Charlotte's chatter I deduced that it was lamb from their own farms. Apparently I was destined to visit the lambs, too.

Lest I be giving the impression that Charlotte was hogging all the attention, let me state that at first she tried to make me the centerpiece of the conversation, asking me questions about my life in the West, what I did, where I lived, the people I knew, and the things that happened there. After a long series of monosyllabic responses failed to deter her, I promised to answer all her questions later and turned the conversation by asking her what sights of interest were to be seen in those parts. It was a spur-of-the-moment action and a very effective one. For every expedition she thought of, Sebastien Thierry suggested another, until it appeared as if they were intent on mapping out the next several years of my life.

The lamb and vegetables were replaced by an enormous serving of Floating Island. Creamy and delicately browned, dusted with coconut and nutmeg, it looked absolutely delicious. Occasionally Mother had made something like this; generally, however, sweets had been crude and rare in the West and I loved them dearly, but between what I had managed of the enormous dinner and that constrictive dress, I couldn't take a bite. It was dreadfully frustrating.

"Floating Island always makes me think of *Saint Cloud*," Charlotte said dreamily, poking her spoon into the puff of meringue. "Mammy Lou used to tell me how Grandmamma deMarchand named it that because when Grandpappa deMarchand brought her there she was reminded of a big fleecy bank of clouds."

Aunt Felicité spoke for the first time since we had sat down. "He told her to close her eyes and then had old Carriage Tom stop the coach at the end of the drive so it was the first thing she saw when she opened her eyes. She told me the story many times. Thank heavens she died in sixty-two."

Now, to someone who did not know the Bonneaus, that might seem both a senseless and cruel remark, but my two days' journey here trapped in a carriage with the garrulous Charlotte and the proud Felicité had filled me in on a great deal of Bonneau-deMarchand history. Mother had mentioned *Saint Cloud*—which was always pronounced *Sahn Cloo* —as it was the other big house of the neighborhood, but she had never visited there and knew none of the family, so her information was limited.

Aunt Felicité had made up for it. During our journey she had spoken—mainly to Charlotte, I might add— about the glories of *Saint Cloud*, the famous personages who had enjoyed its hospitality, the unquestionable status of the deMarchand family. From her point of view, one of the main reasons the Yankees had invaded Louisiana was to destroy *Saint Cloud*.

"It would have devastated *Madame* deMarchand to see what they did to her home," Aunt Felicité said with a mournful sigh. "Heaven knows it shortened your dear father's life."

At the far end of the table the old man made a snorting noise.

"I was under the impression that your husband was a casualty of the late War," Jonathan Eversleigh said in the determinedly bland voice of a mischief-maker.

The old man made another snort. Apparently this was a familiar scenario.

"You know very well my Etienne was severely wounded during the War for Southern Independence. He was very weak when he came home, and finding his home destroyed ..." She swallowed heavily, and I felt sorry for her.

"How dreadful for you," I began, but my grandfather laughed and flung his napkin on the table.

"Men hurt worse than he survived. Damned weakling found he'd have to work his land instead of just sitting on it, enjoying its bounty. If I hadn't taken over the land, it would have gone for taxes, and where would your precious *Saint Cloud* have been then?"

Aunt Felicité's face hardened and the grieving widow was gone. Her chin came up, her eyes narrowed, and she looked exactly like her father. "And what is it now? Sitting there moldering and rotting. I tell you, the longer we wait, the harder it is going to be to restore the place!"

"And I've told you it can fall to splinters for all I care. What do we need another house for? *Ombres* is older and better built, and it's always belonged to the Bonneaus."

"*Ombres* is old-fashioned! *Saint Cloud* was a showplace, the finest of its kind, and can be again! I've told you and told you—"

"And I've told you and told you times are hard. There's a depression on, and I won't starve the land to pour money into a house that isn't good for anything!"

The two antagonists stared at each other, their emotions making the atmosphere as cold and solid as the mountaintop ice that never melted. Spoons and coffee cups hung in midair, and while the others looked as uncomfortable as I felt, Charlotte appeared positively frightened.

"Not good for anything? *Saint Cloud* is Charlotte's inheritance! It must be preserved for her and Bastien and their children!"

Charlotte? And Sebastien? They had never shown anything in front of me beyond an easy camaraderie. I glanced quickly from one to the other and found no evidence of passion, or even of romantic affection. Sebastien was regarding the furious figure of my grandfather with respect and a carefully blank countenance while Charlotte was as pale as the snowy cloth. Her eyes had the same skittish look a young horse will get just before it bolts.

"*Ombres* is Charlotte's inheritance. She and young Thierry can live here after they're married," my grandfather said, his eyes staring directly into mine.

I don't know what he expected, if he thought I might challenge Charlotte's right to anything, but at the moment I had few thoughts to spare for a crabbed and opinionated old man. Instead, my thoughts revolved around my cousin Charlotte. Mother had spoken of arranged marriages among the local aristocracy, but I had never dreamed that such a medieval practice could still be followed in this day and time! However, it appeared that it was, and that poor little Charlotte, who had no more real spirit than a goose, was caught in it. Already her hand was shaking, and if this went any further, she would come completely apart.

Pa always said I had an uncomfortable conscience, and it had already gotten me into trouble more than once; on the other hand, Charlotte had been the only one of the family to be nice to me; and even if she hadn't, I could never stand to see helpless things tormented.

"Just a minute," I said, and faltered as everyone quickly turned to me. To face one emotional Bonneau is no small matter; to face three of them, with Sebastien Thierry and Jonathan Eversleigh thrown in, is indeed sobering.

"And what have you to say, miss?" my grandfather asked in icy tones that shocked my backbone into its proper place. If he was waiting for me to object, he could just go on waiting!

"That I don't understand. You were talking about *Saint Cloud* and what should become of it. I thought it was destroyed."

"They tried," Jonathan Eversleigh said before anyone else could speak, and though his tone was conversational, there was an undertone of contempt I didn't quite understand. "But the Yankees were either incompetent or in a hurry, and they bungled the job of firing the place. Most of the old house is still standing."

"And decaying more each year," Aunt Felicité said as if speaking of a dying relative. "And so needlessly!"

My grandfather made an angry sound of disgust,

though whether over his daughter's comment or my failure to rise at his taunt I don't know.

"But of course!" Sebastien cried, and his voice sounded incongruously happy in the tense room. "This solves our problem of where to take *Mademoiselle* Genevieve first. Tomorrow we will make an expedition to *Saint Cloud*!"

* * * * *

I was not overjoyed with the prospect of a visit to *Saint Cloud* when there was still so much to be seen at *Ombres*, but plans for the proposed expedition dissipated the tension hovering over the table, so I fell in with good grace. Charlotte's color returned to normal, and before long she was chattering happily about luncheons and picnic baskets.

"It should be an interesting trip," Jonathan Eversleigh said with more enthusiasm than one would have expected. "What time shall we start?"

"As much as your presence would be appreciated, we cannot expect you to give up your business—" Mr. Thierry began, but to her mother's obvious disapproval, Charlotte overrode him.

"Oh, do be quiet, Bastien. You mean you will really come with us, Mr. Eversleigh? It's your duty, you know."

He smiled lazily. "My duty, mademoiselle?"

"Yes! It's quite a distance to *Saint Cloud*, and you must help Bastien protect us. For all we know, there may be wild animals or brigands or marauding Yankees on the way."

At that, Aunt Felicité objected to her daughter's

romanticism and my grandfather laughed heartily.

"You're a little late, girl, since all the marauding Yankees are now comfortably sitting up at the state capitol trying to tax us all to death, but it's a good idea. Go with 'em, Johnny, and make sure they don't get into trouble. Now take me back to my room. I'm tired."

I was too—and relieved to see the party break up with my grandfather's departure. It had been a stressful day and I could think only of sleep. How I was going to get out of my golden prison did not even occur to me until I got to my room and found a very sleepy young girl drowsing in a chair. After all the hooks and buttons were undone and the luxuriant weight of it was draped over the chaise, I dismissed her, telling her I preferred to brush my hair myself. There were many things about this way of life I could not quite accept.

My face was washed, my hair brushed and braided into a thick plait for sleeping, and I was just crawling into bed, when quite the most dreadful shrieks I had ever heard clawed through the silence. By and all, miners and prospectors are pretty superstitious and I suppose I'd heard every ghost, haint, and goblin story ever told, so for one frightful moment I stood in paralyzed fear of spirits and spooks until reason returned and with it the knowledge that the shrieks were Charlotte's.

By the time I could cover the few yards between our rooms her wails had abated, muffled in Jonathan Eversleigh's starched shirtfront. She clung to him, gibbering in her terror, and he nestled her close, murmuring calming nothings into her ear, but his eyes roamed the room, alert for any danger, and his stance was one of a man ready for anything.

"Mr. Eversleigh!"

"I was just coming upstairs when she came flying out of her room."

I peeked through the open doorway, the hair prickling at the back of my neck. The room looked remarkably cozy; by comparison, mine looked bare. Beautiful furniture, rugs, pretty knickknacks, and paintings on the wall made a striking picture, but I couldn't see anything that would send Charlotte out shrieking as if all the devils in hell were after her.

Suddenly the doorway was very full of people. Sebastien Thierry, still in his evening clothes though minus his jacket, came running from down the hall and Aunt Felicité, regal-looking as ever in a dressing gown of rose-printed silk, rushed toward her daughter, her face taut.

"What is it? *Chere* Charlotte – "

"What is the meaning of this?"

Well gone in wild-eyed hysterics now, Charlotte resisted the efforts of her mother and clung the harder to Mr. Eversleigh. He spoke soothingly to her and, at Aunt Felicité's statement that her daughter should sleep in her room tonight, gathered the slight, trembling figure up into his arms and followed the dowager toward the front of the house.

He might look like a soft-handed dandy, but Sebastien Thierry was no coward. With a gentle "Stand back, *Mademoiselle* Genevieve," he gently pushed me back from the door and stepped in, fists braced for anything that might come and looking more than a little heroic in his shirtsleeves. He opened the wardrobe, glanced under the high, tumbled bed, and peered out the window, then stood perplexedly in the middle of the room.

"*Mon Dieu*, what do you suppose happened? I can see nothing amiss. Did you see anything?"

By now I had joined him, looking deep into the shadows as if some untold horror might lurk there. "Nothing. Perhaps a snake, or a bat?"

"We sometimes do get snakes, but on the second floor – ? I will check. We must be sure you are safe."

Luckily, I had been wearing my dressing gown when Charlotte began to scream, or 1 wouldn't have thought of it in the emotion of the moment. It was made of heavy blue cotton and simply cut, but most demure. I had, however, forgotten to put back on the soft kid slips kicked off but a moment before.

Mr. Thierry's eyes swept over me, and I had never felt so plain or ugly in my life. Hair loosely plaited like a squaw's, a dressing gown with no style or feminine adornment, and shamelessly bare feet sticking out from beneath the hem. It was humiliating. Suddenly I—who had never cared much about clothes before in my life— wanted a lace nightcap and a sweeping dressing gown of printed muslin with ruffles and a train and—

"We must be very sure that you are safe, my dear mademoiselle," he said in a voice suddenly husky, then swept me up into his arms. I was surprised; he might look soft and delicate, especially when compared to the whip-thin leanness of Jonathan Eversleigh, but there was strength in his arms and hard muscle beneath the ruffles. "No snake should ever be so tempted."

He set me down gently with all due decorum on the edge of the bed and was about to set about searching for a clue when I screamed. Charlotte could hardly be blamed for having hysterics; I felt like having some myself.

There in the welter of bedclothes, where it would not be seen when the servant turned down the covers for the night, but would be felt by Charlotte when she crawled in, was a large black bird. Its neck had been broken so savagely that the head had been torn partly off and its blood was seeping slowly into the bed.

Chapter Ten

Without a doubt *Saint Cloud* must have been one of the most beautiful houses ever built. Where there were no scars of fire one could still see what had been white paint, now faded to a thin gray. Great porches encircled both floors, supported by gracefully shaped columns. Built onto a gentle hillside, it was two stories tall in front and three in back. At one time the grounds must have been beautiful, but years of unrestrained growth in this tropic climate had transformed them into a jungle; even the paved yard in the back had fallen victim to the grass, the unglazed bricks split and lifted by deceptively fragile-looking green shoots.

All the outbuildings were gone, with only an occasional charred timber sticking up through the greenery like a headstone. The house itself had fared better, though it had been dreadfully ravished; the entire east side was a gaping wound, parts of the roof were gone, and the whole thing canted a little to the west. Aunt Felicité believed it could be saved, but I wasn't so sure. Such a restoration would probably cost more than razing it to the ground and building afresh.

I followed Charlotte and Sebastien and listened to

their rhapsodies, dutifully trying to visualize the house as they described its having been. We went only a little way inside, Jonathan having declared the floors untrustworthy, but even in the ruined entrance hall I could see that *Saint Cloud* had been a very different sort of house from *Ombres*. Twin staircases had swept upward in a graceful spiral to the second floor; one staircase still rose with the snaggled remains of steps to a ledge that had been a landing. The other was little more than scars on a fire-ravaged wall.

The drawing room was almost intact, and I agreed with Charlotte that the proportions were most pleasing. But it was a depressing sight. Even the winsomely carved mantel bore the marks of an ax, and I wondered at the beasts in blue uniforms who walked like men and wantonly destroyed inanimate beauty.

"Parts of the second floor are quite untouched," she said artlessly. "I haven't been up there in several years, but the last time—"

"You surely didn't go up that front staircase!"

She smiled. "But of course! It isn't as bad as it looks. All it takes is a little courage."

A little insanity, I thought, remembering the rotting, tilted boards.

"But I fear Grandpappa is right; the old place isn't worth saving." Her voice was unemotional. "Poor Mamma."

"Your mother does seem to love this place." I ran my fingertips slowly over the carved face of a cherub that had been split by a deep gouge.

"'Seem? It's the only thing that has ever mattered to her. She married my father to get it."

I looked at her, amazed at her calm statement and rather wishing that Jonathan and Sebastien would come back from their search for a forgotten wine cellar. Once I had wanted to know about my unknown family; now I feared knowing too much that was distasteful.

"Oh, it's true enough. Even Grandpappa says so. He was willing to send her to Paris—Paris!—but she turned it down to concentrate on snaring Pappa. She's always been determined to have what she wants. Grandpappa says that if she had been put in charge of the army, we could have whipped the Yankees in four months. That's how long it took for her to get Pappa," Charlotte added at my questioning look. "Pappa was almost engaged to a d'Arbanville from Baton Rouge, but Mamma wanted *Saint Cloud*, so she put her mind to it and married Pappa and then she was mistress of *Saint Cloud*. And she never got to Paris." She looked at the wreckage around her and her face was tragic.

"Poor Aunt Felicité!" I said, and I meant it. I couldn't imagine wanting anything material that badly and pitied anyone who did.

"That's why she wants me to marry Bastien. He's the only other possible heir, you see, so our children would have uncontested title to this place."

The sins of the fathers ... even unto the something-or-other generation ... I wasn't used to quoting Holy Scripture, but what I could remember of the quote seemed apt. It might have been kinder had the Yankees completely destroyed the house.

"I wonder if they found any wine."

"Oh, there's no wine down there," Charlotte said with a merry laugh. "The Yankees drank everything the first time they came through here. It's the treasure Bastien just can't resist looking for every time he comes. Poor dear, he needs money so badly I hope he finds it."

Surprise on surprise. "Treasure?"

"Some of the household silver. I think the Yankees carried it all away, but Mamma swears the loyal slaves hid it in one of the wine cellars and someday it will turn up again."

"One of the wine cellars?" For heaven's sake, how many wine cellars were there?

"Let's go outside and wait for them. This place is starting to give me the megrims."

I heartily agreed to that, though she chose a strange place to get away from the megrims. Of course, a couple of servants had been sent over from the house with the blankets and baskets so that they would be there when we wanted them. I was not yet used to such treatment, but Charlotte took it in stride, ordering the blankets spread in the shade of an enormous magnolia tree directly in front of the house.

From this vantage point the house brooded over us, seeming to dominate the sky. It was uncomfortable to look at; to compare the memory of grace and charm with the actuality of destruction and decay was horrible, like looking on the face of a once-famous beauty now raddled with disease and stamped with imminent death.

"Mamma has never forgiven Uncle Rouben." Lounging easily on one elbow, Charlotte sipped at a glass of lemonade.

Yet another surprise. I had sensed the antipathy Aunt Felicité held for her poor disfigured brother, but how was it tied in with the ruin of *Saint Cloud*?

"Rouben?"

"I keep forgetting. You don't know any of the family stories, especially those after your parents left. How confusing we all must seem to you! No, according to Mamma—and I suppose she's right, in a way—Uncle Rouben was responsible for the Yankees' burning *Saint Cloud*."

"Is that when he got hurt?" Such a little word for such a dreadful result.

"Yes, saving my life. My nursery was in the east wing, on the second floor, just about there." Her finger pointed to a blank area of sky.

The tale was simple. *Ombres*, being nearer the road, had been taken over by the Yankees for a command post. *Saint Cloud* was a household of women and children, the only men on the place being slaves too feeble or too young to serve either army. Rouben had been acting as a courier, and that night the Yankees were after him, so, being close to home, he ran like a fox to the earth he knew. Since *Ombres* was occupied, he made for *Saint Cloud* and hid in the cellars. Etienne deMarchand was a connoisseur of wine, and his cellars were legendary for their complexity as well as their contents. Before the War he and Rouben had had many talks about the various vintages, and Rouben knew the cellars, secret and otherwise, as well as anyone.

The Yankees went over the house like destructive terriers, but even though they were unable to find him, they knew he was there. They kept guard so closely that he couldn't escape and, finally getting tired of waiting, one night a gang of them surrounded the house. A lighted torch was thrown into Charlotte's open window and her terrified screams woke the household.

Wherever he had been hidden, Rouben heard his niece's cries and rescued her, then plunged back into the flames to rescue her nurse, who had been trapped by a fallen timber.

"Agnes," I said in sudden comprehension.

"Of course. They were always special to each other. Mammy Lou said Uncle Rouben was always trying to buy Agnes, but Pappa wouldn't sell her. Said he wanted to make sure Uncle Rouben kept coming over to talk about wine."

"But why?" I asked and then suddenly understood. Neither of my modest parents had ever mentioned such a practice, but after the War some of the men drifting through the mining camps had bemoaned the loss of the forced compliance of slave women.

"You should see your face, Genevieve! Of course, we were never supposed to know anything about suchlike, but you can't keep secrets on a plantation. Anyway, Uncle Rouben went back for her and saved her life, but one of the walls fell in before they could get out. Even though she was hurt herself, she managed to drag him out of the building and into the cowshed. Of course, the Yankees searched everywhere, but Uncle Rouben was so badly burned and so covered with ash and soot they thought he was just another darky and left him alone."

It was an ugly tale that left me queasy in the stomach. Fires had been no stranger to the slapped-together mining towns where I had lived, and I had seen their aftermath. No wonder poor disfigured Rouben inspired such hatred from his sister and such devotion from the servant girl. I was sorry Charlotte had told me, for it cast an uncomfortable shadow over the day.

"Now you know all our little secrets and skeletons, Genevieve, it is time for you to keep your promise."

I looked blankly at her. Her hat discarded, Charlotte lay sprawled on the grass, staring up at the sky, her childish position unseemly in a woman grown.

"Promise?"

"Last night. You promised to tell me about the West."

And so I had. After the previous night's horror, I was surprised she remembered anything, but then Charlotte was turning out to be a surprising person.

"Well, what do you want to hear?"

"Everything! What you did, what you wore, where you lived – everything!"

So I began to tell her everything, censoring the worst bits and softening it a great deal. As I dislike dwelling on unpleasantness, I concentrated mainly on the happier aspects of life in the rough-and-ready mining towns. As I talked, I watched Charlotte's serene face and marveled.

Last night she had been in hysterics so violent it had taken her mother and Jonathan the best part of half an hour to calm her down. Sebastien and I had been left with the cleanup of the horror that had been left in Charlotte's bed. Of course, we had not actually done anything, since there were servants to do the work. Neither were we really needed to supervise, as Agnes was there running things with her usual calm, but Sebastien had seemed to think that some representative of the family should be there, so we stayed while wide-eyed servants carried away the grisly reminders and brought in fresh linen and a mattress taken from one of the guest rooms.

It was a disturbing time, one not made any easier by the servants' superstitious mumblings. Even Agnes's carved face was troubled, and she muttered something about a bird in the house meaning a death to come. It had been very late before I finally convinced Sebastien that I was none the worse for my experience and that all I needed was sleep. Somehow I felt he was disappointed that I, too, hadn't dissolved at the very least into a good spate of tears so he could hold and comfort me. I was sorry not to please him, but it was too late and I was too tired.

After that, none of us had really thought the next day's expedition would still be on, but Agnes had carried the information along with our *petit dejeuner* that Mademoiselle Charlotte expected us to be ready to leave at ten. I was ready at nine-thirty, not out of any particular enthusiasm for a trip to a ruined house, but to be sure that I was not again stuck with a slug of a horse. Charlotte's opinion of my skill, however, appeared to be little better than Jonathan's, and I was assigned a docile enough gelding who, though too old for any real frolics, was still far above Jeb Hall's ancient mare. I thought jealously of Jonathan's spectacular bay.

On the other hand, perhaps the choice of this staid animal was all for the good, since this was my first experience on a sidesaddle and a very uncomfortable one it was, too. I sat perched precariously with both my legs most illogically on one side of the horse, the skirts of my habit draping almost to the ground, and all that kept me from sliding off was my right leg hooked in a most cramped position around the horn. It all seemed dreadfully insecure, as there was no way to get a grip on the horse itself, only the saddle; fashionable women must put a great deal of trust in their harnessmakers!

" – then when Cowface Charley said that he'd found the poke in Emmaline's petticoats—"

"Surely a most unconventional place to be prospecting, Genevieve," Jonathan said, and sat gracefully on the blanket equidistant between Charlotte and me. Sebastien was less politic and stretched out, leaning on both elbows at the edge of my skirts.

"Oh, Genevieve has been telling me the most fantastic stories of her life in the West!" Charlotte's eyes were glowing as she sat up and pushed at her tumbled hair.

"And have you been telling your little cousin the truth, Genevieve?" Jonathan asked. In the depths of his probing green eyes I could see the reflections of that sad little cabin, of all the sad little cabins where I had lived, of the dirty towns and the rough miners and Big Billy Johnson's body sprawled across a floor of raw boards. Amazingly enough, over the last few days I had thought little of the realities of that existence, and to face the ugliness of them was almost like a physical blow.

Did he really think I would tell sheltered little Charlotte some of those things?

"Mostly, Jonathan."

Yes, we were all on a first-name basis now, ever since Charlotte, on the ride over, had gotten irritated by Sebastien's constantly calling me "*Mademoiselle* Bonneau" or "*Mademoiselle* Genevieve" and had declared that since we were all related in some form or another we must call each other by our first names. Sebastien seemed delighted, and Jonathan agreed readily to Charlotte's pretty pleading, but there had been a devil of unholy amusement lurking beneath his smile. I could almost hear him congratulating me.

"Did you find the treasure?" I asked sweetly.

Jonathan flashed one of the shimmering smiles that transformed his face. "If you count dust and cobwebs as treasure, we found a great deal of it."

"Indeed," I said, delicately pulling a trailing cobweb from his sleeve, "you both seem to have accumulated all you could carry."

"Our wealthy cavaliers," Charlotte laughed. "With dirty faces! You'll have to wash before we can eat. Cato! Get some water from the well," she called, never turning around to see if her orders were obeyed or not.

"That's the only treasure that's ever been down there," Jonathan said, trying to dust off the worst smears.

"Jonathan does not believe in the treasure." Sebastien was smiling, but there was an edge to his voice. Despite adherence to Charlotte's demand for first names, there was no love lost between those two.

"You're right; I don't, and if you start digging away in there like you did this afternoon, you'll have the entire place down around your ears."

"Nonsense! *Saint Cloud* is structurally sound."

Jonathan splashed his hands and face in the bucket Cato proffered, then waited until Sebastien had finished doing the same. They could be dangerous, these two men, despite their well-cut clothes, expensive boots, and—in Sebastien's case, at least—ruffles, and there was a quarrel brewing between them. I had seen so many fights start up almost every night in every saloon; quick, tempestuous arguments that blew up over nothing and more often than not left both men dead or injured. Violence was never attractive, but the thought of it here, in these civilized surroundings, was obscene.

"How many cellars are there?" I asked loudly, hoping to provide a diversion.

"Seven," Jonathan answered tersely.

"That we know of. Cousin Etienne was a clever man."

"Not clever enough to put adequate shoring under the house when he started digging his little rabbit warren!"

Charlotte put a delicate hand on his sleeve. "Jonathan, what are you saying?"

"I'm saying that this crumbling edifice to a vanished way of life is a danger to life and limb."

"That may be your opinion, sir, and old *Monsieur* Bonneau's as well, but in spite of both of you, *Saint Cloud* still stands!" Sebastien had abandoned his lazy sprawl and had moved to a sitting position that somehow resembled a catlike crouch.

"For how long? One good blow from a hurricane and it'll fall in on itself like a house of cards."

"Do you really think so, Jonathan?" Charlotte asked with melting eyes. "Poor Mamma!"

"And so it should, so all of you can get on with your lives instead of fighting about a rotting hulk that's nothing more than a – corpse of a dead dream, left over from a dead world." There was bitterness in his voice, and for a moment the mask of charm was stripped from his face, giving a glimpse of darker, more painful emotions. "It's the land that matters, not the house."

In a man of lesser breeding, Sebastien's look would have been called a sneer. "That is easy to say when you have none."

Whatever that meant, it was too much. Danger flashed green from Jonathan's eyes and his voice became very soft. "You go too far, Thierry!"

"Stop it, both of you!" I shouted in my most authoritative voice, but it was too late. They had already scrambled to their feet, each barely concealing his pleasure at showing open hostility toward the other. Frantically, I looked around for something to stop the fight. More than once I had laid a scalp open with a handy bottle in hopes of preventing worse bloodshed, but at the moment there was nothing within reach. Even the bucket of water had been carried away by a conscientious servant.

I scrambled backward, determined to yank the blanket out from under them and hope that the shock of a fall would break this dreadful spell of bloodlust.

Once again I had underestimated my cousin Charlotte. At the last moment before blows would start flying, she stepped between the combatants—something that, remembering other fights, ones with knives and guns, I would never have done—and faced Sebastien squarely. Her delicate face was pale with tension and her eyes flashed dark fire.

"Stop it! Jonathan is right, Bastien, just as is Grandpappa. I never really saw it until today, but it is true. *Saint Cloud* is a dream, a dream of a time that is past. Now I forbid you to fight about it!"

Slowly, fists lowered and the bloodlust withered. In a few moments a wide-eyed Cato came to straighten the blankets and serve the hampers of sandwiches and wine and fruit. Through some strange kind of unspoken communication, Charlotte and I agreed that the peace could be kept only by separating the men, so for the rest of that interminable afternoon one of us was talking to one of them at all times. Our diversion worked, but there was still a heaviness in our midst, a tension as ominous as the faraway roll of thunder on a muggy day.

Chapter Eleven

O ur expedition to *Saint Cloud* was the subject of very careful conversation at the dinner table. Despite the constant flow of talk, you could almost feel each word being measured and considered before it was spoken. No mention was made of the near-fight, and Jonathan, being his most charming, managed to make an amusing story out of their explorations in the cellars.

Dinner that night was less formal, and though we had all changed, it was into day clothes. I wore a simple gray muslin, which, though pretty, looked provincial next to my relatives' exquisitely ruched and braided at-home gowns. As I had not worn this particular dress before, both Jonathan and Sebastien complimented me on my appearance, to which Aunt Felicité waspishly remarked that she was glad to see I chose something more suitable to my recent bereavement.

I could have told her that neither Pa nor I held with the custom of wearing one's grief on the outside, or that the practice of formal mourning was all but unknown in the West, but she was in such a mood it didn't seem too smart to say anything. After the excitement of the night before, she had been horrified that Charlotte was determined to continue with her plans. And when we returned, seeing Charlotte in the best of spirits and all of us on a first-name basis, Felicité's mood had darkened. She had spent the day terrorizing the servants, trying to find out how that bird got into her daughter's bed, and her failure to gain any information had so increased her irritability that even her father moved gently around her.

The dinner, though not as complicated as the night before, was delicious. We used the same beautiful china and ornate silverware, but this time there were only half a dozen or so pieces—what the Bonneaus would probably consider the bare minimum. Despite the delicious food, I ate sparingly; the gray dress was nowhere near as tight as the golden one, but it was still confining and I had no intention of being too full to enjoy a dessert! My self-control was rewarded when Aristotle, the butler, brought in a towering creation of cake and strawberries and thick cream. Sebastien called it a *gateau des fraises* and I enjoyed every crumb!

When dinner was through, my grandfather leaned back and drummed his fingers on the table. "It's too early to retire; what do you say to some entertainment?"

When Louis Philippe Montreaux Bonneau made a suggestion, it was treated as an order, so we all trooped obediently into the drawing room, where Charlotte seated herself at the piano. Once, when I was a small girl and Pa had been riding the crest of his funds, a concert pianist had come through whatever town it was and Mother had insisted that we go. I had never heard such playing before and when it was over had cried and refused to leave, thinking that if I stayed, the man would have to go on making such beautiful music. Since then I had heard all kinds of piano players, from bad to worse to truly awful, with the latter predominating, but never again had I heard the quality of that long-ago concert artist.

Not until Charlotte began to play. I don't know if she was really of concert ability or not, but to me she was at least the equal of that forgotten famous man. Sitting as still as a baby deer, I watched her fingers move agilely over the keys, and I had never envied anybody anything the way I envied her ability to create such wondrous sound.

When the others began to talk in low tones behind me, it was very annoying.

"My dear *madame*," Sebastien whispered, "is there any news about the perpetrator of that horror last night?"

"None. I've talked to everyone and no one admits knowing anything about it."

"Did you really think they would, Felicité?" my grandfather asked dryly, hardly bothering to lower his voice. "They never betray their own."

"You're assuming it was a servant," she hissed. "We treat our people well. Why would one of them want to do something like that?"

"It would have to be a servant," Jonathan murmured. "Or, by a very long chance, an intruder. The bird had not been dead very long and we had all been at dinner."

"Or someone very late in coming down," Aunt Felicité said poisonously, and I could feel—literally feel—her eyes blazing at my back.

There was a moment of tense silence where the sweetness of Charlotte's melody intensified rather than masked the tension in the air. Sebastien gasped at such a direct accusation, and even my grandfather harrumphed uncomfortably, but I kept my eyes firmly on the piano. Such a vile accusation could only be ignored or answered in blood. Though my fingers longed to claw at Aunt Felicité's smug, hateful face in righteous fury, I won the hardest battle of my life and pretended I had not heard.

"If you mean me, *madame*," Jonathan said in an ominously low rumble, "I assure you I am innocent. Your niece is my witness."

It was a gracious, courageous gesture on his part, and only later did I begin to wonder if he had been defending me or using me.

When Charlotte finally finished, too short a time later, I felt as I had when I was that small girl, wanting it never to end. I was begging her to play again when our grandfather, his lips curled in a sardonic counterfeit of a smile, spoke to me. "*Mademoiselle* Genevieve, it is now your turn. I believe you once earned your living by ... music."

It was that tiny, insulting pause that angered me. My chin rose defiantly, and I would have stalked from the room in a fury had not Charlotte grabbed my hand.

"Oh, that would be wonderful," she cried, her face alight with enthusiasm. "I should dearly love to hear you sing. Please say you will, Genevieve, please!"

Now I wished I hadn't been so greedy about that strawberry cake. To sing on a full stomach is difficult, and to sing when you are emotional is even more so, but I was so angry that nothing could have stopped me from showing off in front of those insufferable Bonneaus!

"I will," I said easily, "if you would be so kind as to play for me."

"I doubt if my daughter would know any songs you sing," Aunt Felicité snapped frostily, but we ignored her; and after a whispered consultation in which we discovered a mutual love of Stephen Foster, Charlotte began to play the tender chords of "Gentle Annie." It was a very sentimental song, but I sang it straightforwardly without any of the dramatic trills or tears the saloon audiences demanded. Charlotte kept on playing, and without a pause we went through "Camptown Races," "Laura Lee," and "Oh, Susanna!" Then Charlotte swept on into a singularly sweet version of "My Hopes Have Departed Forever."

"I'm sorry," I murmured. "I don't know that one."

It was a bold-faced lie such as I had never told. "My Hopes Have Departed Forever" was one of the favorite sentimental songs of the miners and I had sung it many times, but right now it was too close to the way I felt.

"All right," Charlotte said, easily running a series of chords before starting in on the melody of "Ellen Bayne." "What about –

Her voice trailed away and her fingers were still on the piano as all attention focused on the doorway.

Rouben stood there, a small puppy cradled in his good hand and three more at his feet.

"What is the meaning of this?" my grandfather growled, ignoring his son entirely and looking directly at Agnes, who was trying unsuccessfully to pull the poor thing away.

"I'm sorry, sir," Agnes said, her face alive with fear. "He heard the singing and I just couldn't stop him."

Something else for the Bonneaus to lay at my door; apparently they believed in keeping Rouben completely out of sight and I had unwittingly played siren.

"You are supposed to keep him quiet," Aunt Felicité sneered.

For heaven's sake, he was her brother, not some barn animal! I looked at the hard faces of father and daughter, then at Rouben's poor ravaged one. This confrontation must have been a part of life here, for the other three all looked away, their faces uncomfortable.

"But he is being quiet," I said, "and any performer loves an appreciative audience. Please, Agnes, could you help him to that chair in the back?"

She looked at me with wide eyes but steered the pitiful creature toward the back of the room while Aunt Felicité sputtered in indignation.

"You are presumptuous!" the old man snapped, and his daughter, her tongue at last finding words, spat, "You should be ashamed of yourself."

"I am only ashamed that such presumption should be necessary!"

I would have said more, but wise Charlotte crashed

down on the keyboard and into a vigorous version of "Ring de Banjo." From there we went on through "Ellen Bayne," "Little Jenny Dow," "Come Where My Love Lies Dreaming," "Our Bright Summer Days Are Gone," "I Dream of Jeannie With the Light Brown Hair," "Sweetly She Sleeps," "My Alice Fair," and finally, as my voice was about to give out, "Beautiful Dreamer."

All the time I sang, I watched Rouben. He sat quiet and still, puppies draped around him like flowers, absorbing every sound. At first I wasn't too sure that he was really listening, but then I saw the tears rise and fall from his vacant china-blue eye, and spill down his cheek with the slow regularity of spring rain; and I began to wonder just how much he did understand of his situation.

When Charlotte began "Ah, May the Red Rose Live Always," I shook my head and pleaded fatigue, knowing I wouldn't be able to sing the line "Why should the beautiful ever weep, why should the beautiful die?" while looking at Rouben without breaking into tears myself.

"Oh, Genevieve, just one more!"

"No, Charlotte, as much as we would enjoy it; Genevieve has sung quite a bit," Jonathan said firmly.

"And so exquisitely," Sebastien exclaimed, rising to grab my hands and kiss them. "I have never heard such a beautiful voice!"

My grandfather nodded grudgingly. "You sing pleasantly." Coming from him, it was high praise.

Charlotte's eyes were still on Jonathan. "Genevieve doesn't mind. She must have sung for much longer when she was working in a saloon!"

"Perhaps." Pouring a glass of chilled water from the silver cooler, Jonathan handed it to me, perforce making Sebastien release my hands. I had been unobtrusively trying to obtain their freedom, so the glass of water was doubly welcome. "But surely," Jonathan continued with one of his sudden, devastating smiles, "you do not mean to equate your grandfather's drawing room with a saloon?"

"Very well," she said petulantly, "but I did enjoy it so."

The chair in the back of the room was empty. Agnes had taken Rouben out through the service door.

"So did we all. Where did you learn to sing Stephen Foster so exquisitely, Genevieve?" Without seeming to be rude, Jonathan detached me from Sebastien's side and escorted me back to my seat.

"Pa and I lived for a while in a boardinghouse in Deadwood. One of the other boarders was recovering from a broken leg. He had been in a minstrel show back east until the silver fever hit him. He taught me a lot of songs." I could close my eyes and see Ezra Kingsley's gentle wrinkled face. He had been so kind to a funny-looking girl trying to find a way to support herself and her father, too, if need be. A hastily dug tunnel had collapsed, breaking his leg, and he had sworn that he'd never go mining again. But...

"A real minstrel? How exciting! What happened to him?"

"He left," I answered shortly, but those two words

could not express the pain and abandonment I had felt that summery morning when, his leg healed, he had left, saying he was going to give mining one more try. "I never heard of him again."

"Well," Jonathan said, detaching himself from the wall, "he certainly taught you well."

"Indeed!" echoed Charlotte and Sebastien, but my aunt and grandfather were stolidly silent.

"You are all very kind, but it is Charlotte who should receive the compliments. You play so beautifully—"

"Don't you?"

"I don't play at all."

"Then I shall teach you."

Her spontaneous offer touched me. I should have loved to learn, loved to know her better, but my course was set. Already *Ombres* and its inhabitants were affecting me in ways I had not foreseen.

"Thank you, Charlotte, but there won't be time. I will be leaving in just a few days."

That night there were screams and hysterics again. Even after Sebastien and Jonathan had carefully checked her room for any further horrors, Charlotte had a dreadful shock when, in search of a cooler robe, she opened her wardrobe and found her favorite gown of rose-colored muslin ripped and slashed as if by a savage beast.

Chapter Twelve

Aunt Felicité thought I did it. The others might have too, but they were less obvious in their suspicions. Despite Charlotte's determined cheerfulness and courage—and even more determined championship of me—those were unhappy days at *Ombres*. I would wake each morning wondering why I put up with it, why I didn't just up and go, but each day there was something that made me stay.

Usually it was Charlotte. She was so sweet to me, like the sister I had always longed for, and when her eyes turned dark with the remembered horrors, I would feel very angry and protective of her. In spite of my good intentions, I mentioned leaving less and less often.

While Aunt Felicité was all but openly hostile to my continued presence, my grandfather and I maintained a civil and uneasy truce. We watched each other warily, alert for any weakness, any indication of the next move. In him I saw what Pa could have been had he not been afflicted with his twin weaknesses of drink and gambling, and I wondered what kind of person Louis Philippe Montreaux Bonneau could have been if he had had some of Pa's gentleness. I did not let my thoughts show, however, and kept my guard up, for he was capable of sneak attacks.

"Genevieve," he said suddenly one night at dinner, his voice cutting like a whip through the general talk, "your looks and your voice won't last forever. What do you intend to do then?"

I looked blankly at him, holding my cards close. "I suppose I shall follow the family trade, sir."

The others held their breath as he asked, "Family trade? What the devil do you mean?"

"I shall become a gambler, as your son did."

That night he left the table early without staying for the music. Charlotte and I had formed a habit of playing and singing as we had my second night at *Ombres*. Charlotte would play a different piece each night and tell me what it was called and who had written it. Then I would sing, teaching her some of the songs from the West. On the whole the melodies were simple enough that she caught onto them quickly and could play them without written music.

Jonathan and Sebastien made an enthusiastic audience, offsetting the grim-faced chaperonage of Aunt Felicité and my grandfather. After that first night Rouben always joined us, slipping into the back of the room through the service door. He would sit quietly, the tears streaming from his blank eye, until Agnes appeared to take him away when the music ended. I know that his father and sister were aware of his presence, but they gave no sign that he existed. It touched me that Rouben enjoyed the music, though I didn't know how much until the night of the storm.

It had been uncomfortably sultry since our visit to *Saint Cloud*; the others complained about it and I thought I was going to die, either melted by the heat or suffocated by the thick, muggy air. When the impending storm finally broke, though, I almost preferred the waiting. In the mountains we had storms—noisy, quick rains or deadly-quiet snows that could bury and kill entire towns—but I had never experienced anything like that vicious, wind-driven rain, the incessant lightning flashing from black to white to black again with staggering rapidity, and the booms of thunder that sounded like dynamite going off.

The rain started to come down not long after we returned from a short ride to Dead Man's Bayou—a thoroughly awful place of dark water filled with slimy trees—and it intensified to a genuine storm during dinner. It was still growing as we went to bed, and when, in the middle of the night, there was a frantic pounding on my door, I was sure it was to warn me that the house was coming down.

"*Mademoiselle*?" Agnes's voice was strained and the flaring candle she carried accentuated the sloping planes of her face, giving it a skull-like look. "Will you help me, please? It is Monsieur Rouben."

"Of course," I said instinctively. I couldn't have said anything else; her eyes were agonized.

"It is the lightning. He is frightened of it. Usually I give him some laudanum when there's a storm, but he's been so much better lately." The bitter hope in her voice was tragic. "He is very upset. I thought maybe if you could sing to him…?"

I wouldn't have called it upset. Once, in some nameless town, one of the miners ended a two-week drunk by getting whiskey-crazed; it had taken four men to tie him down after he had started screaming and fighting and flinging himself against the walls. Rouben Bonneau hadn't had anything to drink, but he was in the same condition.

There were a number of lamps in this comfortably appointed room, and in their light I could see a bruise starting to spread across Agnes's cheek. Despite the bright lights and tightly drawn curtains, there was no way to block out all the lightning, and each time it flashed Rouben was like a wild animal, his good arm flailing and his china-blue eye staring in terror.

I certainly didn't know how much good Agnes thought I could do, but I was willing to try. Holding out my hand, I began in a quavering voice, "Gone are the days …"

Outside the world turned white and Rouben roared with fear, his swinging arm catching me a sharp blow along the side of my head and sending me sprawling against the wall. He was not strong enough to deal me a truly dangerous blow and I was more startled than actually hurt; in such panic he would be much more likely to hurt himself than anyone else. That thought propelled me off the floor. I grabbed his arm with both hands and held it tightly in a restraining position my father had taught me years before.

It was a strange posture in which to sing, but I didn't

think of how comical we must have looked until later; nor did I—as another alleged later—choose my song with that vision in mind. It was merely the first I could think of.

"Come where my love lies dreaming–"

By my third song he no longer struggled when the lightning flashed, and by the time I had sung nearly all the Foster I knew, Agnes and I had gotten him tucked into bed. Agnes made a dose of his laudanum mixture and he took it with very little fuss, though it was another hour before he finally drifted off to sleep. I continued singing, softer and softer, until that staring eye fell closed and his breathing became deep and regular. By then I had sung every ballad I ever knew at least twice and even a few of the naughtier ditties slowed down until they sounded like ballads. Despite repeated sips from a glass of water Agnes had handed me long ago, my throat felt as if I had been swallowing parched sand and I was as tired as I had ever been in my life.

"He will sleep for hours now," Agnes said, gently smoothing the covers around him. Her voice shook. "Thank you more than I can say, *mademoiselle*. You are too good to be a Bonneau."

I wasn't too sure I had heard her correctly and would have questioned her, but a strong arm went around my shoulders and a deep voice spoke gently in my ear.

"You're exhausted. Let me walk you to your room."

"Jonathan! How long–?"

"Since just too late to pick you up from against the

wall. And outside the door. I heard the two of you talking as you passed my room. That should answer all your questions."

"Except why you stayed. He was as good as a baby."

"And the storm is still going. Rouben can be dangerous, Genevieve. He is still a Bonneau."

"So am I. And so are you."

"Only remotely, thank God. My father was Uncle Louis's cousin, if you must know. They were in love with the same lady and my father won her. Uncle Louis never spoke to him again. Not until the War, at least, and everything was different then."

"Sounds typical." I could not help yawning, but there was more I wanted to learn, more I wanted to ask.

No, that's not quite true. Somehow the intimacy of the darkened hall, the muted roar of the dying storm outside, the iron strength of his steadying arm around my shoulders, created an atmosphere of coziness, of intimacy I had never known before, arousing new feelings that I didn't quite know what to make of, but which felt so very good. I didn't want the moment to end.

Jonathan left me at the door of my room, admonishing me to sleep. I didn't need to be told that and was horrified to find on awakening that I had slept nearly until noon. The story of what Charlotte called my "heroism" had been told all over the house and I could go nowhere without seeing its evidence.

Aunt Felicité tried to turn the event to her ends, of course, and said again and again that this was proof Rouben should be locked away, though to do them credit, no one else paid much attention to her. Charlotte was full of admiration, and Jonathan, keeping quiet about being there himself, echoed it. Even the servants regarded me with more respect.

"That was a brave thing to do," my grandfather said grudgingly. "Were you afraid?"

"I probably would have been, if I had stopped to think. I didn't."

"Such a heroine," murmured Sebastien, his eyes glowing with a warmth that was just short of worshipful.

Sebastien. I didn't know what to do about Sebastien. There was nothing improper to his behavior—quite the contrary—but something about it both alarmed and pleased me. He was quite unchanged in his manner toward Charlotte, remotely affectionate and kind; no, the change was toward me. He had always been polite and kindly in that exaggerated and overblown Southern way and still was, though with a difference. Had I not known that he and Charlotte were to be wed, I would have sworn he was courting me. It was a pleasing thought, to be courted by a man so steady and dependable, a rock who didn't change according to whim. Charlotte's safe and predictable future seemed quite enviable.

"You must be joking," she said when I told her. We were sharing the swing out under the big live oak tree, enjoying a rare moment of solitude; Jonathan was closeted with our grandfather on some business matter or another; and Sebastien had been pressed as escort to Aunt Felicité on some local visits. Charlotte had been pressed, too, but she had resisted. "I can think of nothing duller," she added with a theatrical shudder.

I would have told her that dull can sometimes be highly desirable, yet I held my tongue knowing she wouldn't believe me.

"He is so proper," she went on, eyes focused on the horizon. "He would never understand if I should want to do something exciting, like dig for the *Saint Cloud* treasure. He digs happily for it himself but would think it exceedingly odd that I should like to try.." She turned to me with a glowing face. "Genevieve, let's do it!"

"What?"

"Dig for the *Saint Cloud* treasure. We could do a great deal of exploring and still be back well before supper."

It was dangerous, I told her, it was foolish and a great number of other things, but nothing made any difference. I soon saw that she was going with or without me, and almost before I knew it, I found myself being hurried into my habit and riding off toward *Saint Cloud* in Charlotte's wake.

Somehow the old house looked different in the afternoon light. The storm had washed the greenery and refreshed everything, making the house seem even more bedraggled and forlorn. Had it been up to me, I would have turned back then and there, but Charlotte was determined, so I followed. Living in the West, where danger was an ever-present part of life, had made me respect instinct and my instinct told me to stay with Charlotte.

We had no sooner entered the decaying hall of *Saint Cloud* when Charlotte said something about there being shovels under the stairs and dashed forward into what must once have been a hidden cupboard. The floor collapsed so quickly that there was no time to call a warning before Charlotte vanished from sight.

Treating the old floor as if it were rotting lake ice, I lay down flat to spread my weight and crept to the edge of the hole. Luckily the drop had not been far—a mere eight feet or so, which I could have managed with ease— but I could see no way of getting out once down there. It was shadowy inside the old house and even more so in the cellar. Had Charlotte not been directly below the hole, I should have had trouble seeing her.

"Charlotte!" I shouted, and could almost feel my heart start to beat again when she stirred and feebly called my name. "You've had a bad fall. Is there anything broken?"

"I don't think so," she said after a moment. "Genevieve, I feel so strange."

"Don't try to move. I'll come down."

"No, don't ... you've got to get help." She was speaking in short bursts, gasping as if she were in pain. "Get Jonathan. He's with Grandpappa ... Jonathan ..."

Strangely enough, my mind had been running along the same lines. I hated to leave her, but it would be difficult for me to get her out of there—if I could at all— and if I rode fast ...

"I'll get him," I promised. "I'm on my way to *Ombres* right now."

As it turned out, I didn't have to ride that far. I flung myself on horseback, which was no mean feat in that dratted sidesaddle contraption, and set off for *Ombres*, whipping my startled mount into a gallop. He probably hadn't hit such a stride in years, but at least he was easier to move than Jeb Hall's old mare.

The crown of what they of this flat country called a hill was the unofficial halfway point between *Saint Cloud* and *Ombres*. I came over it like the cavalry, shamelessly laying the whip across my mount's haunch, just in time to spot a stolid figure riding directly toward me.

"Genevieve!" he cried, and for an irrational moment I was disappointed to see that it was Sebastien. "What is going on? At the stables Bellerphon said you and Charlotte had ridden out without an escort—"

I wheeled the poor pony around with a jerk. "Charlotte's hurt! Come on!"

He asked no more questions, and together we flew back to Saint Cloud. As well as I could, I shouted the facts at him and urged him on.

It turned out to be easier to rescue Charlotte than I had feared, for the cellar in which she lay was easily accessible by a fairly strong staircase from the ruined kitchens, but I could not have done it by myself. Charlotte had swooned, which was probably a blessing. A quick check revealed that she had been correct about no bones being broken, but she was so pale and lay so still that we were alarmed.

With no small effort, Sebastien carried her up from the cellar and, with an even greater effort, managed to mount his horse— Charlotte still in his arms—with only a fair amount of assistance from me. I told him to go on, that I would catch her mount and ride ahead to *Ombres* to give the warning.

It wasn't quite a lie. My poor old gelding was a little winded and Charlotte's horse was loose; she had been in too much of a hurry to hunt treasure to tether the creature properly and it had pulled free to go munch on some giant exotic shrub. The excuse of having to catch the horse gave me a few moments alone to go back into the house and check on something that had been bothering me ever since Charlotte had first fallen.

Stretched flat on the floor, I looked again. They had built it to last, the slaves who had made this house. The thick floorboards were sturdy, merely darkened by years and circumstance, but the places where they had been sawn almost through were pale and raw-looking, and when I touched one of them, the powdery sawdust clung to my fingertips.

Chapter Thirteen

There was no doubt that someone had intended the floor to fall in, but I wasn't convinced that this someone had really meant to kill Charlotte until the next day.

Unbelievable as it seemed, Charlotte was up before any of us the next morning. When I came down for a morning ride to take the edge of my still-simmering anger, Charlotte was already mounted on a showy roan and was putting him through his paces in the paddock. She waved cheerfully as I walked by the barn.

Bellerphon, the head stable man, met me at the barn door. He had little use for humans, but according to the family, his rapport with horses was legendary throughout the country, and for that they tolerated what they called his "uppityness."

"Good morning, Miss Genevieve," he said respectfully. "I'll get your horse ready."

"Bellerphon, do you suppose I might have a different horse? One with a little more spirit?"

His black face split into a big grin. "I was wondering how long you would be happy with old Harold. No matter what Miss Charlotte says, you're too good a rider for something as quiet as that. Do you want to pick, or shall I choose one for you?"

For one moment I looked with longing toward Sebastien's fine pale horse, but I dared not ask for it; besides, I should be afraid to try riding it with a sidesaddle. "You choose one for me," I said with a smile.

At first glance I thought it had been a mistake, for he led out a great dull brown beast with a Roman nose and a sullen eye, but once I had been thrown up into the saddle and trotted out toward the paddock, my opinion changed. He might look like a bone-setter, but this hulking horse had gaits like velvet and more brains than some people I knew.

However good he was, though, I knew I was no match for my cousin; Charlotte was the first to say she was not a very good rider, but anyone who could make sitting on a sidesaddle look that easy and that graceful had to be quite good. I watched her with pleasure and admiration. She was a wonder, the best of all a Bonneau should be. The day before she had been lying unconscious in a cellar, having fallen through a sabotaged floor, and today here she was out riding.

"Good morning, Genevieve."

"Good morning, Jonathan. I'm glad to see you."

"A statement that warms my heart." Jonathan smiled and pulled his magnificent bay up close, making my poor brown steed look even more unprepossessing. Despite myself, his smile sent shivers down my back.

"I want to apologize for my behavior last night," I said. "I shouldn't have shouted like that."

He shrugged. "You weren't shouting at me. Besides,

if that woman had accused me of trying to hurt Charlotte, I should have done a great deal more than yell. I take it you haven't told her about your grandfather's offer?"

"I wouldn't tell anyone about that," I said grimly, "but she's partially right, I think. I don't know—"

"Genevieve, what are you talking about?"

I don't know why I told him. I had intended to keep it as my secret until I knew more, but his clear green eyes seemed to reach into my soul and pull out answers.

"Where Charlotte fell, it wasn't an accident. The floorboards had been cut."

Then he had to know the whole story; I told him the little more I knew, knowing almost for the first time the relief of sharing a burden. His face darkened as he listened intently.

"I don't know why or who ... or even who they were trying to hurt," I finished, struggling to put half-formed thoughts into words. "No one could have known Charlotte would go across that part of the floor first."

"It could have been meant for you."

I almost asked him who would want me hurt or dead, then stopped. "Or you. Or Bastien. Or someone else who goes to *Saint Cloud* that we don't know about."

"That's reaching, Genevieve." He dropped lightly from his horse. "I think I'll ride over to *Saint Cloud* and look around. I'll just get a lantern. Stay out of your aunt's way, will you?"

"You don't really think she'd stoop to anything so crude, do you?"

"Not personally. But she certainly did hurl some ugly accusations at you last night, and I have a theory about people who say things without provocation."

"She rounded on you pretty well too."

He grabbed the reins tightly. "It is a habit with her."

"Jonathan, I can understand why she dislikes me so, but what does she hold against you?"

"You don't know, do you?" The green eyes looked up quickly, the hard question in them quickly replaced by a disturbing irony. "Because if anything happens to Charlotte before she marries and has children, I am Uncle Louis's sole heir."

"You! But—"

"As long as you are out of the succession, of course. Rouben and Felicité are taken care of no matter who inherits."

"Good morning!" Sebastien called, waving from the stable door. "Just let me get *Ma Blonde* and we will all ride together!"

Jonathan swore under his breath. "Genevieve, stay with Charlotte; keep Thierry with you if you can and ride in any direction except toward *Saint Cloud*! I want to get a look at those boards. I'll wait until you all leave before I get that lantern and start out."

I would rather have gone with him, and even then I was still telling myself it was just to find out the truth about Charlotte's fall, but I agreed. It was more of a shock to find out that he was the heir after Charlotte; somehow I hadn't pictured him being that closely aligned to the family, despite my grandfather's dependence on him.

Leading his beautiful horse, Sebastien joined our group with a hearty chuckle. "I see you have captured the good Bellerphon's respect, Genevieve. Caesar is one of his pets."

"Caesar?" An apt name, considering the beast's Roman nose.

"He was the last horse Uncle Louis bought for himself before his health failed," Jonathan said, stepping over to rub the beast's nose. "Caesar was the last of Rose Park's famous stable."

How chagrined the old man would be to find I was riding his personal horse! I also wondered why the mention of Rose Park, whatever that was, should bring such a melancholy look to Jonathan's finely hewn face, but all thoughts were cut short by Charlotte's terrified wail. We all turned as one to see her normally well-behaved pony rearing and twisting, nearly unseating Charlotte. Then it bolted, taking off madly across country. Apparently the reins had been pulled from her hands, for Charlotte was unsteady in the saddle and her hands grabbed wildly for support.

Had I been mounted on my usual slug, I could never have done it; in fact, had I stopped to think about being in one of those accursed sidesaddles on an unknown horse, I would never have done it, but instinct overrode all considerations and I put an ungentle heel into Caesar's brown flank. He started forward with an enthusiastic bound that nearly unseated me and—perhaps fortunately—wedged my leg into the saddle horn so firmly that I couldn't have fallen off had I wanted to.

Behind me I could hear the men mounting and urging their horses forward, but by that time Caesar was far ahead and had no idea of being approached by anything or anyone. Whatever Rose Park was, it had had magnificent stables if Caesar was any sample. When a four-bar fence lay across our path, he cleared it as if it weren't there. He was amenable enough about going in whichever direction I chose as long as I didn't try to brake his speed, which was just fine with me—though I did hope there were no more fences; that was an experience I didn't care to repeat. I lay across the dull brown neck and whispered encouragement as Caesar drew ever closer to Charlotte.

"Genevieve!" my cousin gasped as we drew abreast. She was on my offside, but if I stretched, I might be able to reach the loosely flapping reins...

I nearly had them in my hands when suddenly her mount shied, jumping to the side, and both Charlotte and her saddle came off in a heap almost under Caesar's thudding hooves.

Jonathan and Sebastien were not far behind, and both of them reached Charlotte before I did. First I had to calm and stop Caesar—no small task, as he was still fresh—and finally to extract my leg from that dratted saddle. By the time I was free and Caesar safely tethered, Jonathan and Sebastien were involved in the delicate task of freeing Charlotte from the tangle of her saddle.

Sebastien gently braced her shoulders while

Jonathan tugged at the saddle, then suddenly, making a sign for silence, showed me the broken girth. It had been neatly sliced nearly all the way through.

"Jonathan?" Charlotte whimpered, then began to cry in earnest, her cries rising to hysterical heights until, over Sebastien's protest about such ungentlemanly action, Jonathan gave her a hearty shake and gathered her into his arms.

It was a dreadful replay of the day before. Once again I rode ahead to warn the house while the men came more slowly, Charlotte this time cradled against Jonathan while Sebastien rode anxious guard.

I hated approaching Aunt Felicité, especially after our ugly scene the night before, but aside from one blistering look she paid me no attention in her rush to get things ready for Charlotte's arrival. Servants bustled back and forth with bandages, and Bellerphon himself was sent for the doctor.

Wishing nothing more than to stay out of the way, I stepped into the drapery-shrouded drawing room and collapsed into a chair. It had been an unhappy choice; the big piano stood there as a mute reminder of happier times.

"It would seem that the Bonneaus have had a streak of bad luck since you came here."

I looked wearily into the hooded eyes of my grandfather and tried not to hate him. "Through no action of mine."

"I wonder."

"Are you accusing me?"

"Don't fly into my face so quickly. No, I am not accusing you. It merely seems odd."

"A great number of things here seem odd," I returned, "but it is not my place to question them."

"Have you reconsidered my offer?"

"No, I have not." I looked at his pale bony face and tried to feel pity for such a poor specimen of humanity. "And I will not. If it were not for Charlotte's desire for me to stay, I should have gone by now."

He rubbed a thin finger along the side of his nose and looked at me as if trying to read the cards I held. "So you think that by cozening up to her you'll get a better deal?"

I opened my mouth to scream at him, to tell him exactly how low I thought his suggestion was, but suddenly I was too tired. The excitement of the morning had not left me enough energy for futile exercises. I stood and pulled on my riding gloves. "I had no such idea, but I cannot expect you to understand."

"Come back here, Genevieve," he snapped as I passed his chair, well out of reach of those grasping talons. "I want to talk to you."

"I can think of nothing we have to say to each other," I answered wearily, and closed the door behind me.

It was a relief to get out of the house. In the excitement no one had thought to stable Caesar; he was standing patiently by the veranda and seemed as glad as I to get away. We trotted easily down the drive, and when he turned left at the main road, I allowed him his head. Bitter tears filled my eyes and I couldn't care less where we went.

How easy it would have been just to keep going, letting Caesar carry me ever farther away from *Ombres* and all its sadness and hostility. Of course, tempting as the idea was, it was impossible. There was no way I could leave Charlotte until these mysterious attacks were cleared up—and besides, I would have been foolish to go off and leave my few belongings and my almost fifty dollars. On top of everything, the Bonneaus would probably charge me with horse-stealing!

Not that Caesar, who was trotting steadily down the road with an easy gait, wouldn't be worth taking that risk for. If I hadn't already owed my grandfather so much money, I might have thought about offering to buy him.

"May I join you?" Jonathan reined back on his bay, bringing his gallop down to Caesar's trot.

I hadn't even heard him approach. In the West such carelessness could have cost me my life instead of just my pride. Since there was no hope of concealment, I brushed away the tears and their damning tracks as if it were the most natural gesture in the world. "Of course."

"Are you crying?" he asked in an odd tone. "I've never seen you cry before, even when you thought that bully was going to attack you."

Big Billy Johnson. How long ago that seemed.

"How is Charlotte? Is she badly hurt?"

"More shaken up than anything else. She was incredibly lucky."

"But how much longer can she stay lucky? The next time—"

"According to your aunt, there won't be a next time. She's dosed Charlotte with laudanum and is sitting in her room like a guardian dragon."

"So she's safe enough for now, at least. Who...?"

"I have an idea," Jonathan said grimly.

"You do? Who?"

"I'll tell you when I'm ready. By the way, I apologize."

"Whatever for?"

"For the horse in Three Mile Creek. Seeing you take out after Charlotte ... I had no idea you could ride like that."

In spite of myself, I laughed. "Neither did I. At least, not on one of these silly sidesaddles. Jonathan, what do you do? Where is your home? Surely you don't live at *Ombres* all the time." Suddenly I felt I had to know. If he was close to solving the trouble about Charlotte, it would not be long before I could leave *Ombres*, so this might be the last time we could talk alone together. I looked into his green eyes and felt incredibly sad.

"I live in New Orleans mainly, and as for what I do, I'm a gambler. You shouldn't look so shocked, sweet Genevieve! It was you who called it the family trade, remember? Anyway, I'm not the kind of gambler you know. I gamble in business—buying and selling commodities—crops, racehorses, that sort of thing. Believe me, it's as much gambling as cards or dice. As for my home, that was it."

Caesar's meandering had led us down country lanes until we stood on the crest of a hill overlooking the burned ruins of another great house. Nothing of this one had survived; all that could be seen were some charred timbers poking up through the enshrouding greenery. In another decade it would be hard to tell that there had been a house on the site at all.

His face was grim and set. "That was Rose Park. It was a beautiful place. Not so grand as *Saint Cloud* or *Ombres*, but still beautiful."

"And the Yankees burned it. I'm so sorry."

His voice held no trace of emotion. "No, the Yankees didn't burn it; I did."

Chapter Fourteen

It was during Reconstruction, when things were so hard and there were no laws to protect us Southerners. The Yankees and the Negroes could do no wrong, but a native born Southerner couldn't do anything right. The Yankees raised taxes until almost no one could pay them. Uncle Louis managed to save *Ombres*, of course, and *Saint Cloud*, because Felicité was his daughter and *Saint Cloud's* land is the best in the parish, but Father couldn't raise enough to meet the taxes on Rose Park. He tried – sold off everything of value, but somehow the taxes were always just a little more than he could pay, and each year they were more than the year before."

We were sitting under an enormous magnolia tree; the horses were tethered nearby and the still, hot air was filled with the sounds of birds and insects and small animals scurrying about their business. Somehow Jonathan had lain down with his head in my lap; he was looking away, his eyes fixed on the ruin of his home, and I had to consciously restrain myself from stroking his dull gold hair in comfort.

"Surely the taxes couldn't have been that much."

"You don't know what it was like then after the War.

White Southerners had no rights at all. We found out that one of the Yankee officials' wives had seen Rose Park and wanted it, but they didn't want to pay a fair price. If my father couldn't meet the taxes, they could get it for that and so they did. Uncle Louis was very kind; he took my parents to *Ombres*."

"And you?"

"I was a hot-headed young rascal. I couldn't stand the thought of some thieving Yankee living in my home. I couldn't do anything about the land, but the night before the tax sale, the last night the place was legally ours, I snuck back here and burned every building on the place." His voice was dark with remembered emotion and I could see a grieving, angry boy, too young for the army but too old to stand by and do nothing, deliberately setting fire to the only home he had ever known, careful to see that he destroyed everything.

"What did they do about it?"

"Probably would have hanged me if they could have caught me. Uncle Louis declared that I would be safer away from Louisiana for a while, so he sent me West. I stayed away and traveled around for a couple of years, until things loosened up here, until that Yankee and his wife left. Then I came home."

"And your parents?"

"They were both dead by then." He spoke casually and without emotion, but when he turned to look up at me, there was still pain in those beautiful green eyes. "Mother died soon after I left. She had been frail for years; I don't know how she survived the War, but she did. She just couldn't stand the loss of her home."

"Poor thing."

His hand found mine and held it, our fingers interlacing. It was a graceful hand, a strong hand, and it felt so very good curved protectively around mine. "Father left *Ombres* after she died ... for all that they were second cousins he and Uncle Louis never did have much in common except that they both loved Mother. He went to another cousin in Baton Rouge, but he never adjusted to city life. Cousin Marius said he just faded away." Jonathan was silent a moment and I could have wept for the empty loneliness in his face. Then, with a determined burst of energy, he sat up and looked over the land, seeing it as it was now, not as it had been.

"Uncle Louis had been very kind to us, and when I finally did come back, it was a shock to see how much he had started to fail. It was the least I could do to help him, to get things set aright."

Suddenly all the blighted dreams, all the lost chances, seemed too sad to be borne and my eyes filled with tears. "It's so sad. If only he had known – "

"Known what?"

"About me. About Mother and Pa. If he had known where to find us." I couldn't articulate my chaotic thoughts of Pa playing the repentant prodigal in truth, of all of us returning to *Ombres*, perhaps to face the horror and deprivation of war, but certainly to build up a strong family household that could survive anything.

"Don't build dreams on falsehood, Genevieve," Jonathan snapped, and though his tone was harsh, his eyes were full of pity. "He knew. He could have found you any time he wanted. Your mother wrote him not long before she died, begging him to look after you."

"And what did he say?" The words were like pointed stones in my mouth.

"He wasn't nice about it. He forbade any of the family to write or acknowledge that they had heard from her. Your name wasn't mentioned again until he started talking to the lawyers about his latest will. I'm sorry, Genevieve," he said gently.

So none of my dreams were going to be left me. It was just as well. Dreams can be dangerous things; they distort your thoughts, distract you from the really important things. I had been just like Pa, living in a rosy future that had no relation to reality.

Jonathan was staring out over the land and his face was unreadable. "Lately I've been hungry to own land again."

"Who owns Rose Park now?"

"I don't know. It went on the market a few months ago, but I wouldn't want it. This place is dead. This area is dead. They'll still be fighting the War and dreaming of lost glory a hundred years from now. I want to go someplace that's looking to the future, a place where a man can use his talents and make something …"

He kept talking, but I didn't really hear him. Instead, I was hearing my father, always talking about the next town, the next state, the next game, always chasing the rainbow. And then I saw my mother, encouraging, then agreeing, and finally just accepting, growing older and quieter and ...

I shuddered when I realized how the life I had been halfway dreaming of was so very likely to turn out identical to my mother's. Madness even to think of putting my life in any hands but my own!

"Where are you going?" said Jonathan when I dislodged him by scrabbling to my feet.

"I want to see how Charlotte is." I made sure to stand still and shake out my skirts casually, so that my departure should not have the appearance of a retreat.

He asked if I wished him to escort me back to *Ombres*, and when I said no, he neither protested nor tried to follow me. Fool that I was, I was vaguely disappointed that he didn't.

* * * * *

"Genevieve?"

Pulled from a nostalgic reverie of a highly idealized West quite unlike the one where I had really lived, I looked up into Sebastien's smiling face.

"Bastien! Is there anything wrong? Does Charlotte want me?"

"Always thinking about Charlotte! So very admirable, but so very intimidating to one who seeks your company alone. You make me feel so very unwanted. May I join you?"

After that, what could I say? I had intended to spend the afternoon alone, sorting out my chaotic thoughts and, pleasant company though Sebastien was, I did not welcome his intrusion. Still, I slid over on the swing and made room for him.

It was late in the afternoon and the worst heat of the day was over; spots of sunshine poured sideways through the tree above and splattered over all underneath. After riding I had changed into the first thing that had come to hand, and even though it had been cleaned, my simple day dress from Denver was no match for Sebastien's elegantly cut trousers, fine coat, and embroidered vest. I felt exactly like what I was—a poor relation.

"What were you thinking of with that faraway expression, *ma petite?*"

"Home. The mountains. The mining towns."

"And this makes you so sad? Then you must think of them no more. You must think only of things that make you happy." He spoke earnestly and reached out, but this time I was prepared, and my hands were carefully disposed deep in the folds of my skirt.

"Did I look unhappy? I guess I was just homesick."

"But *Ombres* is your home now."

I shook my head. "No. This is just a visit. I shall be leaving soon."

"That is an eventuality I must do my utmost to prevent." Once again he extended his hand, seeking one of mine; then, when mine stayed resolutely unavailable, he casually draped his arm along the swing back. "This is not a bad place to live. Right after the War so many left, and now that we are in this depression so many more are leaving, but I feel this is the time to stay, to build –"

I almost shivered. His words were so similar to Jonathan's, but as he kept on talking I saw the immeasurable distance between dreams and dependability.

"I cannot share *Madame* deMarchand's enthusiasm for *Saint Cloud* in an economic sense. Without slaves, the old plantation system is too expensive. Someday I should like to rebuild the house, of course, but the money will have to come from trade, not the land."

"Trade?"

"You sound surprised, *chere* Genevieve."

"I am. I hadn't thought. I mean, you've been here for so many days and – "

"You thought I had wealth? No Southerners have wealth, Genevieve; the Yankees have seen to that. I am associated with a mercantile house in New Orleans—Villiers. Does that offend you?"

He sounded so earnest I couldn't help laughing. "That you work for a living? Of course not! Why should it? I've worked most of my life and shall probably work the rest of it too."

"I took the job at first simply because I could get it and my family had to eat, but I was as surprised as anyone to find that I liked it. I like putting things in such a way that people want to buy them. I like deciding what stock the store will carry. Before long I hope to buy in as a partner, or to start my own if the owners do not wish to take me in. I want to expand – to have a Villiers in every town in Louisiana. or at least in every parish. Oh, I know it will be slow at first, that each store will take time to build –" He talked on, warming to his subject, describing in detail his plans for selling his theories of expansion to the older, more sedate partners of the firm, then how he wanted to start building a chain of stores one at a time.

I can't say I found it interesting. I don't know enough about stores to understand the business of selling, but Sebastien did; he seemed to know it very well. No overnight fortunes, no neck-or-nothing gambles for him; he wanted to build slowly on a solid foundation. As he spoke, his enthusiasm showed in his voice, and in spite of my ignorance I became as excited as he did.

We talked until a little boy came out to bring us in to supper, which was its own particular brand of discomfort. In order to join us, Aunt Felicité had entrusted the sleeping Charlotte to her maid, an enormous woman who had been born a slave and who was as much a part of the family as her mistress. The supper table was the perfect spot for Felicité to unleash her stored-up vitriol.

Beginning with me, she worked her way around the table, flinging only slightly veiled accusations as easily as if they were salt. I was behind the accidents to Charlotte because I wanted more of the inheritance; at one point during her diatribe, I started to tell her in no uncertain terms the true state of affairs, but a certain gleam in my grandfather's eyes stopped me. I would not seem to use his horrible offer in a bid for sympathy. I would not!

Warming to her subject, Aunt Felicité insinuated in the most delicate way that I was scheming to steal Sebastien, and when he protested, she absolved him as being a mere boy led astray by a wild Western witch. He protested more loudly at that, but my angry relative then switched her attack to Jonathan, saying that we were working together to do her daughter out of her rightful inheritance and that she, Felicité, would fight to the death to prevent an adventuress and a bastard from taking over *Ombres*.

My grandfather slapped the table with a sound like a pistol shot. "That will be enough, Felicité! Marianne Eversleigh was a lady of spotless reputation and I will not have her memory defamed."

He looked capable of doing murder. So did Jonathan. His face was white and taut and wearing an expression that I was extremely glad was not directed at me! He put down his knife and fork, dabbed at his lips with a napkin, and stood up, all the while never taking his cold eyes off Aunt Felicité, who had gone pale herself.

"I think my obligation to you is completed, Uncle Louis. I shall be leaving—"

"Sit down!" the old man roared. Even as old and sick as he was, Louis Philippe Montreaux Bonneau could muster enough power to stop Jonathan in midmotion. "Sit down, Johnny. Please. I loved your mother, and even though you aren't my son, you've served me better than either of my own children did. Felicité will not overstep herself again." His voice hardened even more, making the last sentence more of a threat than a pronouncement.

Aunt Felicité puffed up like a pigeon, then looked down at her plate and did not raise her eyes again. Jonathan hesitated for a moment, then sat down stiffly. His face was still hard and wary.

Suddenly I couldn't stand it anymore. Murmuring a hasty "Excuse me," I stood and tried hard not to run from the room. The old man called out orders to stop, but I ignored them. It was only Jonathan's hand on my arm that finally brought me to a halt at the base of the stairway. His face was still taut, but there was a kindliness in his eyes.

"Are you all right, Gene?"

His use of my old name almost broke my self-control. "Yes. I just had to get away from them."

"Just a little longer, Gene," he said cryptically, and then Sebastien was beside us with anxious inquiries. At last I had to accept his escort to my room, but I would not linger in conversation.

During one of Pa's flush times, I had eaten too many chocolates and had been nauseated for hours. Now I had had too much of the Bonneaus and I felt exactly the same way, though in more of a mental than a physical sense. All I wanted to do was lie down and be quiet and think of places other than *Ombres*. My thoughts, however, defiantly dwelled on Jonathan and his odd comment. I fell asleep vowing to ask him about it at the first opportunity, not knowing that it was to be our last private conversation for days.

Chapter Fifteen

The next days were not easy ones for me. Charlotte, only slightly invalided by her latest mishap, rejoined us with smiles and gaiety and jokes about her clumsiness. Apparently Aunt Felicité had been ordered by her father to be less unpleasant and, unable to comply, she retreated into a silence that was unbroken except by the most necessary and monosyllabic communications.

I should have rejoiced that Charlotte's spell of bad luck seemed to be over and there were no new mishaps, but my attention was focused on the observation that all of Jonathan's attention was on Charlotte. Our old foursome was dissolved, for the two of them were always together, walking, talking, laughing. He refused to let her ride, so almost every afternoon they disappeared in the buggy for several hours. I should have been happy that things were disposed so felicitously, but my unruly woman's heart jumped every time I saw Charlotte place a proprietorial hand on his arm or Jonathan bend an obedient head to catch her breathless chatter. The worst thing was that I didn't know if my unsettled feelings were caused by sheer jealousy or the sneaking suspicion that the lack of fresh accidents proved at least some of my aunt's accusations.

My days were not empty; Charlotte managed to squeeze

in a few piano lessons for me and insisted that I practice. I enjoyed those sessions at the piano, though I doubt anyone else in the house did. Sebastien was there, too, his attention to me in direct proportion to Charlotte's ignoring of him. I no longer imagined that there was any romantic attachment between them, but Aunt Felicité's daunting looks every time Sebastien sought my company reminded me of her plans. How it must have galled her to see the upstart remote relations she detested oversetting everything she had planned!

Charlotte bloomed during those days, becoming quite a belle. She laughed, she enchanted, she refused to allow any glumness around her. At mealtimes, the few times we were all together, she prettily begged Jonathan and Sebastien for stories of life in New Orleans and charmed me into talking even more of the West. I had heard of love transforming people; apparently it had worked its magic on Charlotte and on Jonathan, too, for he smiled a lot, usually at Charlotte, and was seldom more than an arm's length from her side. I tried very hard to be happy for both of them and began thinking seriously of leaving. I need not—could not—stay any longer.

I announced my decision one sunny afternoon in the drawing room. Charlotte and I had just finished a music lesson with Jonathan and Sebastien as a more polite than honest audience. Charlotte made a voluble protest, calling on the gentlemen to second her, then argued with me until her maid came to call her to change for supper. She followed obediently, but turned at the door to tell me she would talk to me later.

I was sure she would, and the prospect was not pleasing. Charlotte was used to having her own way, but then so was I. I was afraid what remained of my visit was not going to be pleasant.

* * * * *

"I said I would help you when you left," Jonathan said, and I jumped. After the music lesson I had decided to take a short walk in the shabby garden before dressing, knowing there were only a few more days at most to enjoy what had been my father's home. Once I left I would never return.

"It's very kind of you, but I don't want to be a bother."

"And do you think that anything concerning you is a bother?" He was standing behind me, so close that I could feel the warmth of him. "Genevieve ..."

In spite of everything, my heart leaped in my bosom. Taking my courage in both hands, I made myself turn and face him. The gentle sunset light sculpted his strong face into sharp planes and angles; I remembered how he had burst into that small, ugly cabin the night Pa died and saved me from Big Billy Johnson like some sort of avenging angel, and wondered that I could ever have thought him ugly. There was strength in that face, and compassion, and charm – and I couldn't trust him! For days he had been dogging Charlotte's footsteps like a faithful shadow, and now he was looking at me with an expression in those clear green eyes that could melt stone.

"I should appreciate it if you could arrange for a carriage to take me to the nearest railroad station."

His hand cupped my cheek. "What's wrong, Genevieve?"

"Nothing. You know this was to be nothing but a visit. I've stayed too long as it is. I've decided that it's time for me to go back home."

"Back to those saloons?" he growled. "Back to those godawful mining towns? Back to men like the one you shot?" His voice was suddenly harsh and his hands locked painfully on my shoulders.

"No, I miss none of those. I thought perhaps Kansas City or Denver or San Francisco. Concert singing. Stephen Foster." I was babbling; I knew it and it angered me. How could I let this man make me lose control?

"Admirable. You would be good at it. If that's what you really want to do, Genevieve, I'll help you. Just wait a little longer."

The promise in his voice was tantalizing, and it was difficult to keep my composure, especially when his hands were tenderly working their way along my shoulders. "I have already stayed here too long," I said. "I must go."

His hands were like fire against the bare skin of my neck. "I thought we had an agreement, Gene. Why didn't you talk to me about going West before making such a dramatic announcement?"

"You've been busy." I really didn't mean to sound so waspish, but the slivered words were flung and I couldn't call them back.

"Are you jealous?"

"Of course not! Why should I be?"

He was smiling, and the light in his eyes ignited a wild fire in my blood I had never felt before.

"Because of this," he said, and, pulling me close to him, kissed me.

Mother used to kiss me, her dainty lips barely brushing my cheek or forehead; I don't remember Pa ever kissing me, but some of the miners, too far gone in drink or ego, had tried, their unshaven cheeks and loose lips groping over my face until I could fight them off. None of that, however, had been anything like this!

Jonathan's lips were soft, as I had dreamed them to be, and they touched mine gently, almost hesitantly, then more and more firmly, as if he were unable to restrain himself any longer. At first I resisted, holding myself rigid against his embrace, but as the warmth of him bathed me like a fire, I melted and molded myself against him, denying even then that I had longed for this ever since he had helped me out of that accursed tree my first day in New Orleans, and perhaps even before that.

His lips were moving now, exploring the contour of my jaw, tasting the sensitive skin under my ear, awakening in me avalanches of feeling I had never known. I could not even respond, could only stand there and let his hungry lips taste my eager flesh. At that point I would have agreed to anything he said, forgetting Charlotte, forgetting my own life, forgetting everything!

Unfortunately he did stop, pulling away suddenly and pushing me back as if I were distasteful to him.

Knowledge of and shame at my own vulnerability crashed over me; I hated him for having put me in such a spot and myself even more for allowing it.

"That's all, my dearest Gene, or I won't promise to be a gentleman. Damn it, woman, do you know how hard it's been to keep my hands off you? How much I've wanted to do that ever since that first night? You're wonderful, Gene. You'd just lost your father, you shot the man who broke into your home, and you still had manners like a reigning queen. I knew then only you would do for me."

His voice was weaving just as potent a spell as his lips had. It was like slogging through an icy stream to make my words come.

"Is that why you spend so much time with Charlotte?"

The green eyes narrowed, this time without humor. "You are jealous! Do you love me, Genevieve?"

I had to look away. "Charlotte—"

"I should have done it differently. I should have known – Genevieve, please wait just a little longer. I can't explain just now, but just believe me, my darling; you are the only one for me." He pulled me close in an embrace again and his voice grew husky. "We must be married quickly, my beautiful one. I don't know how much longer I can wait."

My head just fit into the curve of his neck, and for one moment I let myself listen to his beautiful words, pretending that they were real, that I belonged there. It was one of the most exquisite moments of my life and I enjoyed it fully until reality, never very far away, was dragged back by his next words.

"We'll have a grand life, Gene. There are lots of opportunities just waiting for us in the West. There are fortunes to be made. Just as soon as I get something going, you'll live like a queen."

"Let me go." Firmly, deliberately, I pushed away from him. "You should stay with Charlotte. You'll make a fine pair, dreamers both of you."

"What are you talking about, Gene? You can't tell me you don't feel something for me."

"And you can't tell me you don't feel something for Charlotte."

"Leave Charlotte out of this! I can't – What's the matter with you? You enjoyed that kiss as much as I!"

Thoughts and ideas and memories boiled in my head, but I couldn't put words to them. I pushed him away and maneuvered a rosebush between us. It was easier to think when he wasn't touching me.

"And that's my tragedy. Yes, I enjoyed it—Heaven help me— but I've seen a lot of men like you. My own father was one. Lots of talk, lots of hope, and that's all. You charm women, you seduce them with words and leave them with nothing."

"That was your parents. It won't be like that with us!" Jonathan snapped in very unloverlike tones.

"How do I know that? I don't want to end up like my mother. She died before her time. She worked herself to death to keep food on the table and a roof over our heads, all because she trusted my father to take care of her and he didn't!"

His face was rigid with anger, and even in the dying light of day his eyes shot green sparks of pure fury. "Are you comparing me to your no-good sot of a father?"

"Yes!" I shrieked, caught in a maelstrom of my own emotions. "You're all alike, you charming men. You get what you want, and the women who love you get nothing!"

"Except love."

"And what good does that do? If love means an empty belly and having to sleep in a field when it's cold and rainy because you don't have enough money for a room, and having to save every penny just for food to eat and clothes to cover yourself with, I've had love and I've had all I can stand!"

He reached for me, but I stepped backward and evaded him.

"Leave me alone, Jonathan!"

"This isn't the end of it, Gene," he called after me.

A strategic retreat, I have been told, is not the same as running away. I'd like to think that this was a strategic retreat, but in my heart I knew it was a complete rout. If I had stayed, I could not have resisted the insistent pull of the man. Damn him! Charlotte adored him; why did he think he had to have both of us?

I stopped at the base of the stairway, puffing like I had run halfway up a mountain, half-hopeful and half-fearful that he would follow me. When strong hands closed on my shoulders, I didn't know whether to run or to be relieved.

"*Cbere* Genevieve! What has disturbed you so?"

I turned and looked into Sebastien's handsome face. Concern was written all over his solid features, and his dark eyes—so like the Bonneau eyes—were alive with worry.

"I was in the garden.Something alarmed me," I added weakly.

"A fright like that cannot be good for the nerves. Please – rest and compose yourself for a moment."

If he had heard what transpired in the garden, he was too much of a gentleman to contradict my words, which in all good conscience were the truth. Instead, he placed a very correct hand on my waist and, taking my arm with his, led me into the shadow-shrouded drawing room.

I allowed myself to be swept along and settled into a delicately carved chair, even as I protested that such cosseting was unnecessary. Paying no attention, Sebastien genteelly arranged my skirt so that he could pull the companion chair—a bigger version of mine with arms tipped by carvings of a woman's head—close to me. He had already changed for the evening, and the odor of the bergamot scent he favored drowned out the night scents of *Ombres*.

"Bastien, it was really nothing—"

"If it affects you, it cannot be 'nothing," he said gallantly, and tenderly clasped my limp hand. I made no effort to draw it away. "You must be more careful with yourself, dear Genevieve. You are too precious. I must tell you –"

I would like to say that I had an inkling of what was happening, but I thought it was only the prologue to one of his stories, which he had already begun to repeat. Sebastien Thierry was a born storyteller, with a gift for nuance, mimicry, dialogue—everything necessary to a good story, in fact, except the recollection of how many times he had told it. It wasn't until he slipped from the chair to his knees and pressed my unresisting hand against his moist lips that I realized this was not going to be another recounting of some past glory or future plan.

"Genevieve, dearest and most wonderful of women, I cannot tell you how I feel about you—words have not been made to describe the depth of my feeling. I have but little to offer ... "

Little to offer? A home, a business, a solid future; did he value these so lightly? As he talked on, I tried to look at him dispassionately; he was very good-looking, but had a solidity of build that in a few years would run to fat. He would always be chivalrous, kindly, and stolid; already some of his stories and plans were beginning to seem a little tedious, but life with him would be so blessedly safe and predictable. I liked him; was very fond of him, in fact. If he could never make my blood sing or my knees turn to water, was that not just more proof of his unwavering dependability?

Then he said something that made me wish I had been listening more carefully.

"... and then I am sure your grandfather will relent. And even if he doesn't, we shall manage. Please say that you'll marry me, sweet Genevieve!"

I looked deeply into his pleading eyes. No wild promises, no declarations of how I felt from him, just a simple statement of love and an honorable offer of marriage. I only wished I had listened a bit closer to that part about my grandfather. Well, it didn't make any difference. Sebastien Thierry had offered me a secure, loving future.

"Yes, Sebastien," I said softly, and bent my head to his soft, seeking lips. No passionate embraces for him, not now; he had even waited until my acceptance to aspire to kiss me. It was so very different from—

"Good heavens!" Charlotte's voice floated down the steps. "Haven't you changed yet?"

"I was just on my way up," Jonathan drawled, and my heart shrank to a small, tight fist in my chest. Had he heard?

I don't care, I thought defiantly. I didn't care what he thought about anything!

"You'd best hurry then," Charlotte said with a laugh. It was a sweet musical sound that changed to a terrified shriek.

By turning in my chair, I could barely see the end of the staircase, but it was enough to see Charlotte seemingly flying through space, her mouth open in an *o* of fear, to see Jonathan run up the short flight to catch her in his arms, to see the two of them tumble down and land in a dreadfully still heap at the bottom of the stairs.

"Jonathan!" I screamed, then in the next breath added, "Charlotte!"

We were at their sides in a heartbeat, Sebastien helping me untangle the two bodies. Aunt Felicité, a dressing gown hastily thrown over her unmentionables, appeared at the top of the stairs and started to shriek like a train whistle. Then we were surrounded by people—Agnes, Aristotle, Cato, half a dozen wide-eyed servants; even my grandfather, his face purple from the effort, had wheeled himself from the back of the house.

Charlotte, her face flushed and her hair tumbled, regained consciousness first. It seemed a lifetime since they had fallen, but logic dictated that it could not have been more than a minute by the clock from the time Charlotte fell until she moaned and moved her head. Jonathan took longer to come around, and I had already sent one of the servants for cold water and cloths before his eyes began to flutter.

"Jonathan," Charlotte murmured.

He responded magnificently, raising himself on one elbow despite his ashen pallor and a slightly unfocused appearance about his eyes. "Are you all right, Charlotte?"

She looked absolutely beautiful lying there, her hair and skirts swirling about her, her face delicately pink. My cousin was one of the lucky ones who could come through the worst disasters and look charming; in the same circumstances I should look like a street urchin and probably have a black eye as well!

"You saved my life."

"But what happened?" our grandfather roared. His color had returned to normal and he disliked being left out of control of any situation for long.

"This!" Sebastien snapped. He had climbed to the top of the stairs, and now he stood there like an avenging angel, the two pieces of heavy thread that had been tied across the stair in his hand.

Chapter Sixteen

Another "accident," and it had almost killed not only Charlotte but Jonathan as well. Why now, after there had been none for so long? I put the finishing touch to my hair and took one last look in the mirror.

This certainly was a culture alien to me; another possibly fatal "accident," two people injured, and yet we still dressed for dinner. I couldn't quite understand it, any more than I could figure out who was behind all this senseless violence.

I stopped at Charlotte's room before going down. She had requested my presence, so when I knocked at her door, it was opened immediately by my aunt, who greeted me with a scowl. "I am surprised you have the gall to show your face here!"

"Mamma!"

"Nothing has been right with this family since you came. Nothing!"

I looked at my father's sister and wondered that I should ever have feared her so. Prideful, aging, trapped forever in a world of lost grandeur, of course she would fight for her last thing of value: her daughter. If I could only have convinced her that we had the same goal, but she would never believe me, especially when it became common knowledge that I was to marry Sebastien – he whom she had personally chosen as husband for Charlotte and master of *Saint Cloud*!

"I'm sorry you feel that way, Aunt Felicité," I said with sincerity. "I would like to speak with Charlotte, if I may."

Aunt Felicité drew herself up in a great huff, looking like nothing so much as a pouter pigeon. It was almost possible to see her puffing out feathers. "Most certainly not! I will not have my daughter put at more risk!"

"Mamma, please. I wish to speak to Genevieve." Charlotte's voice was soft, but carried the sound of immutability.

"Charlotte!"

"Please, Mamma." It was not a request, but the demand of a spoilt and pampered child.

For a moment everything hung in the balance, then Aunt Felicité looked at me with hateful eyes.

"It was a black day for the Bonneaus the day Pappa brought you into this house!" she spat, and swept past me, pausing at the door only long enough to say, "I shall be just outside, Charlotte, in case this creature should try to harm you!"

It was as direct an insult as I had ever received, and my hands clenched into fists as the door closed behind her. Only Charlotte's merry laugh—this time tragically weak—stopped me from yanking the door open and giving her mother a few of my own thoughts!

"Can you credit that, dear Genevieve? For all as if

she expects you to murder me in my bed!"

My fists slowly unclenched, and I grasped Charlotte's outstretched hands. "She probably thinks I've tried to already. Charlotte dear, you know it isn't I who's been doing this to you."

"Of course it isn't! I never thought such a thing!"

Such goodness and trust overwhelmed me. "Your mother does. And the others, too, I bet. They'd like to see the last of me."

Real fear blossomed in Charlotte's eyes. "You won't leave me, will you, Genevieve? Not when I need you so much. You're the only one I can trust."

I licked my lips. "I'm not going away. This is hard for me to say, Charlotte, but – I'm going to marry Sebastien."

Indeed, that had not been easy to say, and for more reasons than fear of Charlotte's reaction. It was one thing for a girl to disparage a suitor, to ignore him and make fun of him, but quite another to hear that he who has been promised to her since girlhood is going to wed another. I braced myself for tears, recriminations, hysteria, but Charlotte's angelic expression of delight shocked me.

"You are! Oh, dearest Genevieve, that is wonderful! Now you will stay here forever! Bastien is quite wild about you, you know."

"Has he talked to you about me?"

"No, of course not; he is too much the gentleman for that, but I can see it in his eyes. Genevieve, you have made me so happy!" She sat up in bed and hugged me.

"And you don't mind?"

"No, of course not. I am very fond of dear Bastien, of course, but he is more like a brother to me than a lover. Mamma was always pushing us together whether we wanted to be or not. I am so happy for you!" She smiled, then, twisting her hands together like a little girl, looked up at me with barely concealed joy. "You see, I'm to be married too."

I tried to keep breathing, to keep smiling, not to let Charlotte know what I feared. "You are?" My voice sounded thin and very far away.

She nodded. "It's Jonathan, but of course you knew that," she said with a smile, unknowingly plunging the blade directly into my heart. "He's so wonderful, Genevieve, so brave and so exciting."

And he had been making love to me in the garden not two hours before, the rat!

"When are you going to be married?" I asked, willing my voice not to shake.

Charlotte's eyes slid away. "I don't know exactly. Dear Jonathan is so reticent. I'm afraid I shall have to be most unladylike and urge him on a bit."

"Do what?"

"Urge him on. Not every man is in a rush to get married, especially as quickly as his woman wants. Sometimes we just have to take things in hand and hurry them along. Don't look so shocked, Genevieve; it's quite a common practice. Even Mamma did it."

That made me uneasy; I tried to tell myself that my fear was for Charlotte, that she had so little experience of the world, that she could be so easily hurt. "Charlotte—"

"Now don't you start sounding so prosy! We're in love and we've made such wonderful plans. Jonathan is so exciting! You're happy with Bastien; you aren't begrudging me my happiness with Jonathan, are you?"

It was so close to what I was feeling that I felt a rush of embarrassment and quickly denied any such thing, hugging her tightly as I wished her every happiness.

"Jonathan does love me, you know. He's so dear and so tender. He says he wants nothing more in the world than to make me happy. He says he wants me to live like a queen." She sighed, and her eyes were full of stars. "But I could talk about him all night, just like you could about Bastien. Go on down to dinner, Genevieve; you know what a bear Grandpappa is when he's kept waiting. I'll be all right in the morning. Perfectly all right," she added with a plucky little smile.

* * * * *

Meals were always protracted affairs at *Ombres*; the family liked to linger over aromatic coffee and fruit and talk. That night the conversation consisted mainly of who had tied the cord around the stairs and how whoever it was could be sure Charlotte would trip on it. Of course, Aunt Felicité made her opinions clear, but the rest of us came to no viable conclusion, and when Sebastien shyly announced our engagement, it effectively changed the direction of conversation.

"I should have expected such behavior of you, you hussy," Aunt Felicité all but snarled, but my grandfather merely harrumphed, "So you've decided you want to stay in this part of the world after all."

Jonathan, his face taut and pale as if he were in pain, said nothing. He drank the obligatory toast when my grandfather sent for a bottle of champagne, but his face was averted and I could not see his eyes. What difference did it make? He was in love with Charlotte.

But there was a difference. Something didn't quite make sense. Admittedly, a lot of things about this genteel Southern way of life made no sense at all, but this was different. Leaving the dinner as soon after the grim toasts as was decent, I declined Sebastien's offer of a walk in the moonlight and escaped to my room. I had to think; something was not quite right, but I didn't really know exactly what. Pulling the pins from my hair, I began to brush it with slow, steady strokes. The main question was, who would want to harm Charlotte? Ideally, the answer to that would seem to be me, but I knew that wasn't true, even if no one else did.

So – logically that left only Sebastien and Jonathan. Sebastien needed money to hasten his dream of a mercantile empire; he could have seen Charlotte slipping away from him, decided to romance me and increase my theoretical inheritance by killing Charlotte. There were only two things wrong with that picture – firstly, Sebastien was a very thorough person; the way he talked about his business proved that, and I could not picture his being repeatedly so inept if he really wanted to kill her. And why would he just want to frighten her? Secondly, again being so meticulous he would doubtless know that if anything happened to Charlotte,

Grandpappa's estate would go to Jonathan. Sebastien had no motive.

Then there was Jonathan; my heart contracted as I thought of him. He was in love with Charlotte. What better way to attract a romantic young girl's attention than to create danger and then rescue her from it? But they both could have been killed by that fall tonight. And how could he be sure that she would be the first to come down the stairs? For that matter, if he was so crazy about her, what was he doing romancing me so passionately in the garden?

I groaned and cradled my head in my hands. The more I thought about it, the less sense everything made, especially my impulsive engagement to Bastien!

That at least I had some control over. Tomorrow I would end the betrothal. It was the only right thing to do. The promise of status and security was not enough to imprison myself for the rest of my life in the most intimate of relationships with a man whom I did not love. I would have to leave *Ombres*, of course. Even if I were wanted here it would be too difficult to stay and see the man I did love happy with someone else.

"*Mademoiselle*, I must talk to you."

I nearly jumped out of my skin. Agnes could move as silently as a cat. "Please don't sneak up on me like that."

"I am sorry, mademoiselle, but I did not want to attract the attention of the others." Her face was as hard as her voice was soft, and I sat forward, my instinct singing that she might have an answer.

"What is it, Agnes?"

"You have been kind to *Monsieur* Rouben and I owe you for that. *Mademoiselle* Charlotte is not in her bed."

My heart all but stopped. "Not – but how? Who took her?"

"She took herself, *mademoiselle*. Her maid is bribed not to admit her mother, and a dummy fills her bed. She left as all of you sat down to eat."

"But where? And why?"

A suspicion of moisture glinted in those coppery eyes. "Your cousin wishes to marry *Monsieur* Eversleigh. She has gone to *Saint Cloud* to wait for him."

Something inside me twisted and knotted painfully. "An elopement?" I breathed, but even as I said it, I knew it wasn't true. Again my stubborn mind told me that something did not fit.

"I have said enough, *mademoiselle*," Agnes said shortly, and was gone as silently as she had come.

Damn and blast Charlotte's romantic heart! How could she be so foolish? She wanted to marry Jonathan, so she just forgot about the attempts on her life and rode out to *Saint Cloud* in the night ... Didn't she have any idea of how dangerous it could be? How could Jonathan put her at such a risk?

Or had it been Jonathan?

That thought sent me skimming out of my dress and digging frantically through the room in search of my pants and Pa's old ruffled shirt. They were, along with my cracked old boots, stuffed in the bottom drawer of the armoire behind my shoes, as if they were too shameful to be put with the rest of my clothes.

How strange they felt! Without the encumbrances of skirts and petticoats and such, I felt almost as if I didn't have on any clothes at all. They felt as alien now as my skirts had before; another change wrought by *Ombres*.

There were still people up and about downstairs and I must not be seen. I shinnied down the ivy trellis outside my window instead of risking the stairs, then ran to the stable. Caesar nickered softly and stood patiently while I put a sensible saddle on him; tonight I wasn't in the mood to bother with one of those pesky sidesaddles.

The ride to *Saint Cloud* had never seemed so long and— despite the nearly full moon—so sinister. It took an effort not to let my imagination paint masked riders in every shadow. If there had been anyone at *Ombres* whom I could trust completely, I would have ridden back to fetch them!

There was no one, however, and so I rode on, thinking almost longingly of the days when I had believed that Pa's big old pistol could solve all my problems. I had brought it with me, of course, and reached under my shirt to touch it like a talisman. If I had to use it tonight, I hoped my marksmanship would be better than last time.

Saint Cloud was depressing enough by day; by moonlight it was positively eerie. I tethered Caesar in deep shadow away from the house and crept forward. Where was Charlotte? I didn't dare call out, but I didn't want to enter that house!

With part of the roof and the whole east side gone, there was a fair amount of light inside, but that glimmer of yellow coming from upstairs was from a lantern, not the whitish moon. Charlotte had talked about climbing those stairs before; apparently she had done so tonight, and that meant I would have to as well. I looked up and swallowed heavily.

In a way she had been right; it wasn't as difficult as it looked, but she must have had a better head for heights than mine! Clinging to the wall, I inched up the remnant of stairs and tried not to look down. Charlotte had done this wearing the trailing skirts of a riding habit; my admiration for her grew. Getting back down again was something I didn't like to think about.

Oddly enough, the second floor seemed sounder than the first, or perhaps in the dim light I just couldn't see the weak spots. In any case, I had no trouble getting to the big back room where Charlotte sat.

At one time this must have been the master bedchamber. It was a corner room, and two walls were solid French doors, nearly all their glass gone now, looking out over the tranquil countryside. The walls and ceiling bore traces of decorative paint and carving, and a part of me mourned for such beauty irretrievably lost.

The only illumination came from a lantern sitting in the middle of the floor and turned very low. Its dim light made the room seem that much bigger, the shadows that much darker, but there was enough light to see that Charlotte was alone in the room. I was not too late.

"Charlotte!" I tried to keep my voice low. Sounds carried in the night. "Thank heavens you're all right!"

"Genevieve!" she screeched, and her eyes blazed with

anger. "What are you doing here? You'll ruin everything!"

Chapter Seventeen

Ruin everything? Charlotte, have you forgotten there's someone who wants to harm you? You're in danger here!" I reached out to her, but she jumped up and put the chair between us.

"Go home, Genevieve. Jonathan's coming and you're going to spoil it all!"

Was she so in love with Jonathan that she was blind to her own safety? I wondered, then realized I was in no position to criticize her feelings. "Are you sure it was Jonathan who sent you word to come here? Charlotte, your being here is just an invitation to whoever's been causing all these accidents. They might have just used Jonathan's name."

The anger in her died, replaced with bubbling laughter. "You haven't figured it out. Or maybe you have, and this innocent act is your way of ruining everything for me." Her eyes narrowed coldly. "Greedy, aren't you, my dear cousin? I gave you Bastien; do you have to have Jonathan, too?"

I looked at this new, hard face of my cousin blankly. It was as if solid earth had shifted beneath my feet and nothing was the way it had been before.

"So now you understand. I know it will be Jonathan

coming, because I left a note telling him I would be here. He's worried about someone trying to kill me, too, and he'll hurry right over to save me. He does love me, you know, Genevieve, just as I've loved him for years and years."

"Years?"

"Yes. All my life. When he went away after the War, I thought I'd never see him again, but he came back to me. Then he had to go get you and I hated that, but when he came back, everything was perfect again, except he paid too much attention to you and not enough to me. I didn't mind Bastien paying attention to you. . . . I wanted him to. But not Jonathan."

I was indeed beginning to understand now, and it was making me sick. "So you caused those accidents yourself."

"Of course I did! Did you really think anyone could be so infernally clumsy if they wanted to do me harm? I worried about that, but I had to keep you here – dear Cousin Genevieve. It was very clever of me, don't you think? I kept you here to occupy Bastien and I got all of Jonathan's attention and made everyone think I was a poor, persecuted heroine. Not bad for a few small bruises." She smiled like a self-satisfied cat.

"But why? Surely if Jonathan loved you—"

"He didn't want to take me away from Bastien!" Her voice was acid. "Everyone wants to keep me here, tied to this old place, to this stuffy horrible life! Even you, you who've had it all, told me I should be glad to stay here! Why should I? I want adventure and excitement too!"

With a sinking heart, I realized I was partially responsible for this; I had told Charlotte only the funny things, the exciting things, and left out the grim reality. "It's not all like that, Charlotte."

"No, it's too late now. You're the one who's stuck in this dreary backwater. The family would never let me go if there wasn't someone to sacrifice in my place ... so now it's you who must stay here and raise babies to worship *Saint Cloud* and *Ombres* and listen to Grandpappa's boring stories and live up to the family name. I've done it for years and now I'm getting out. Jonathan ..." She caught her breath. "You've got to go, Genevieve! He'll be here in a minute."

"You're going to trap him in some way." Fragments of the conversation in Charlotte's bedroom came back to me. Maybe I was indeed slow, but surely not stupid.

"Not trap; just hurry things along." She giggled delightedly. "All I have to do is keep him here with me all night long and then he'll be honor-bound to marry me. You're shocked, Genevieve! I told you it was an old Southern custom. That's how Mamma caught Pappa, after all."

I had my doubts about Charlotte's being able to force Jonathan into doing anything he didn't want to do, social ostracism or no, but that didn't seem very important now. Charlotte was ill; she might not be in danger from some unknown assassin, but she was in danger from herself. She was ill in the mind and surely as sick as if she had typhoid.

"Charlotte, you don't know what you're saying.

When you've thought it over, you'll think differently about this – "

Her laughter was now high and feverish. "When I've thought this over? What else do you think I've thought about for years? No, dear Cousin Genevieve, this is the way it's going to be. I don't want him kissing you in the garden anymore!"

"But I turned him down. You didn't hear that part of it, did you? It was you who arranged the fall on the staircase, just so you'd have all Jonathan's attention," I said slowly, memory and reason working together. "And almost got him killed!" I added in sudden anger, remembering Jonathan's poor, pale face and growing bruises.

She shrugged and looked away, trying not to appear guilty. "I didn't mean for him to get hurt. I was just going to stumble and land in his arms. Who'd have thought he'd come running up the stairs like that?"

"Anyone who knew him! This has gone far enough. I'm taking you home right now," I said with more spirit than sense.

Brave words indeed; Charlotte was nearly as big as I, and even though I felt sure of being able to wrestle her into submission, how on earth was I to get her down those infernal stairs and then back to *Ombres*?

She wasn't having any part of it; darting from my outstretched hand, Charlotte ran through the empty French door out onto the veranda, which shuddered and popped under her weight.

"Be still, Charlotte! You'll bring the whole thing

down!" I shrieked and stepped gingerly onto the warped flooring only to jump back hurriedly as it moved beneath my feet.

"Go away or I'll jump," she hissed from the railing. "I promise I will!" In the moonlight her eyes had a wild look and I didn't doubt that now, with the line between sanity and desperation blurred, she would do exactly what she threatened.

I stepped back into the room and tried frantically to think; how ironic that I had come out here to try to save her life and in doing so had, however innocently, endangered it. Whatever was done would have to be done quickly; that veranda wouldn't last much longer, and since we were at the back of the house, where the hillside sloped away, there were three floors between Charlotte and the ground.

"Charlotte!" Jonathan's voice rumbled out of the dark. It was the most welcome sound I had ever heard.

"Jonathan!" Charlotte cried in delight. "I'm up here, darling!"

"Stay right where you are! Don't move! I'm coming for you."

For a moment I felt a rush of sheer fear – not, I am ashamed to say, for my cousin, but for myself. In this state there was no telling what Charlotte would say; Aunt Felicité was already convinced that I was behind the "accidents" that she had been having. After this it wouldn't be too hard for her to convince everyone else.

Well that, as Pa used to say, was the next hand; right now getting Charlotte safe was my main worry. Jonathan

might be coming, but that old veranda was so shaky I
didn't know how much longer it would last. Probably no
one had trod on it in years, perhaps not since the fire,
and it was groaning alarmingly.

"Genevieve?" Her voice was small. "I'm afraid. Help
me."

"All right," I said uncertainly. "If you reach out, I
think ..." I put a timid foot out on the protesting veranda
and, when it gave slightly under me, grabbed the
doorjamb and stretched out as far as I could.

Charlotte reached out to me, too, but she seemed
unable to let go her death grip on the carved post. She
clung to it tightly with one arm and extended the other
toward me. There was still more than a foot between our
fingertips.

"Let go, Charlotte! You've got to come this way
more!"

"I'm afraid! Help me, Genevieve!"

The edge of panic in her voice blinded me to caution.
I let go of the jamb and inched out farther toward her,
my hand stretched out as far as it would go. "Reach,
Charlotte!"

She leaned out until her hand latched onto mine
with an iron grip. The moonlight caught her eyes; they
were full of feral cunning and then, just half a second
before it happened, I knew what she was planning. Using
her hold on the post as an anchor, she yanked me toward
her, and as I neared the rail she sprang forward and into
the house.

Shrieking like a mortally wounded animal, the old

veranda slowly began to tear itself loose from the house and slip jerkily downward.

I didn't scream; it was a useless waste of energy. Instead, I clung tightly to the sagging railing and tried not to think of the broken brick paving three floors beneath my feet. If I rode the porch down I would surely be killed; there was no way anyone could fall that far onto bricks and live.

The veranda stopped sliding for a moment, hanging precariously a foot below where it had stood for so many years. The wood groaned and popped, and even if it was still at the moment, it could be only minutes at the most before it broke free and fell, taking me with it.

I had only two options: the house itself and an aged giant of a live oak tree that grew beside it, both tantalizingly just out of reach. The house was a good five feet away across rotten, tilted flooring. I could never make it in less than two jumps, and I had a dreadful feeling that the slightest move would dislodge the porch completely. I'd never have time for the second jump.

Beneath me the grass-grown bricks looked like silver water in the moonlight. I felt nauseated.

The tree? Even my slight act of turning my head made the wood beneath me protest. The leafy branches were closer than the house, but they were only the tips of the tree, weak little twigs that would never support me. It would take a tremendous jump to reach a part strong enough to bear my weight, and then it would be a gamble; what if this leafy giant were as rotten as the one I had climbed down in New Orleans so long ago? It could send me to the ground as quickly as the porch.

"Gene?" Jonathan's voice was urgent.

Turning my head very gently, I could see both of them in the hallway door, Jonathan struggling toward the French doors, Charlotte flinging herself in front of him, trying to hold him back.

"Jonathan! You did come, my darling—"

"Dammit, Gene, where are you?"

"There's no one here, darling," Charlotte said just as I found my voice.

"Out on the porch. It's falling."

Even in the dim lamplight I could see his face go pale. "I'm coming, Gene. Hold on."

With a sound like a pistol shot, the porch heaved and sank another foot. Now I could see the gaping holes in the side of the house, the splintered wood of the failing joins.

Inside, a wild-eyed Charlotte grabbed Jonathan's sleeve in a death grip. "Let her be! She meant me to be out there! She's the one who's been trying to kill me, darling!"

His face a frozen mask, Jonathan pushed her away from him and dispassionately gave her a solid right to the jaw; Charlotte crumpled quietly to the floor and Jonathan stepped over her body without a second look.

"Don't come out," I cried. "It's about to go."

Bracing himself in the doorjamb, Jonathan held out his arms. "Jump, Gene! Now! I'll catch you."

I froze. How could I hope to reach him? Frantically, I turned toward the tree. If I took a big jump, and the tree wasn't rotten, and a branch didn't stab me, and I didn't hit hard enough to break a rib—

"Gene!" Jonathan shouted, and there was agony in his voice. "Damn you, you've got to trust somebody sometime! Jump!"

The old wood gave a tired sort of sigh, and without thinking, without reason, I leaped forward with my arms outstretched.

* * * * *

Jonathan grabbed my reaching arms just after the planking fell away from beneath my feet, and for one horrible, dizzying moment I swung suspended three floors above the jagged brick and the smashed remains of the old veranda far below, supported only by his strong hands. It felt as if I hung there forever, but it couldn't have been more than a second or two, for at the moment of contact Jonathan flung himself backward, sending us both crashing to the dusty floor, our feet sticking out over all that nothingness. I was tightly wrapped in his strong arms and I knew I was safe.

Chapter Eighteen

I t's a plot! They're working together trying to steal Charlotte's inheritance!" Aunt Felicité's shrill voice floated down the staircase. She sounded almost hysterical, but then she had sounded like that since Jonathan and I had straggled in during the wee hours, a still-unconscious Charlotte slung across his saddle like so much laundry. Aunt Felicité had cursed us, called us devils, and when she found out that Jonathan had actually knocked her baby out! Well, I never knew that a lady used such language. Half the words she used I didn't even know.

"Damned fool woman," my grandfather harrumphed. He looked very old.

"At least the doctor said that with time and care she would recover," I said wearily.

"Brain fever, he says. Old fool. I told Felicité not to marry deMarchand. Bad blood in that family, and don't you scowl at me, Sebastien Thierry. You know as well as I that two of Etienne's aunts had to be locked away."

Sebastien said nothing, but his fingers nervously interlaced again and again with mine. I felt sorry for him. I felt sorry for everyone, myself included. It had been a horrible night, one that was just now giving way to the first grayish hints of dawn.

We all huddled in the drawing room as in a house of sudden death, Sebastien and my grandfather in their ornate dressing gowns and Jonathan, looking weary enough to drop, still in the torn and filthy suit that was mute testimony to his night's exertions. Both Sebastien and my grandfather had been horrified at my scandalous costume, so I had been hurried upstairs to change into something decent. Not that appearances mattered, not after an awakening Charlotte had begun to babble a wild mixture of accusation, fantasy, and supplication that only laudanum had silenced.

"When did you know, Johnny?"

"Almost immediately after we got back. I suspected, that is." He rubbed his eyes slowly, then stretched and took another sip of coffee. "I had no proof until I heard her yelling at Genevieve at *Saint Cloud*."

"You heard everything?" I asked, frantically trying to remember exactly what I had said.

"Such a tragedy, and my darling Genevieve is so much of a heroine," Sebastien murmured, pressing my hands to his moist lips in an excess of emotion. Somehow that made me feel as if I were on a curb rein. Irritated, I snatched them back and, when he reached to recover them, smartly slapped his hands away. There had been no chance for a private conversation with him yet, but at the first opportunity I must speak, must tell him that marriage between us was impossible.

"Charlotte never was the most stable girl in the world; damned deMarchand blood," Grandpappa huffed. "Why didn't you tell us, Johnny?"

That was something I wanted to know myself.

"Because I didn't know exactly what she wanted. I played her little games, trying to figure out exactly what she had in mind. I must be getting old, because she told me all the time that she wanted to travel and have adventures with me, and it was so simple I didn't think that could be all of it. I was afraid she meant to harm Genevieve."

His flat words reached out to caress my heart. I almost spoke then, but my grandfather's harrumph was like nearby thunder.

"I'd like to see her try. Genevieve has all the qualities a Bonneau should have. I want you all to know I've decided to do the fair thing and split the estate between Genevieve and Charlotte. If Anton had had half the gumption you do, girl, it would have all been his anyway. So as long as you remain at *Ombres*, you will be my heiress," said Louis Philippe Montreaux Bonneau at his most regal.

"Sir!" Sebastien snapped. "Genevieve is to be my wife! She will reside in New Orleans with me."

"Of course, you damn young puppy, but she'll stay here until the wedding, and you better bring her down often for visits!"

My heart thudded hollowly, and I looked at Jonathan for some clue, some sign, seeing nothing but set muscles and hooded eyes that seemed to penetrate my soul.

"And as for you, Johnny, I must feel like Father

Christmas, because I've got a little something for you, too. Rose Park is on the market. I've decided to help you buy the place back and get it started up again. What do you say to that?"

For one wild moment I had horrible visions of a future with him so near while I was tied to Sebastien, and then that changed to a different dream, one that he had once offered me and I had been insane enough to turn down. I had what I had come here seeking— not the inheritance, which meant very little to me— but for the first time I was accepted as a part of the family, a Bonneau of *Ombres*, and suddenly it meant nothing at all.

"I say thank you, Uncle Louis, but no. This way of life is dead; I'm going West. I want to build something new in a new land."

"Fool!" the old man bellowed. "Land out west is full of Indians and cutthroats and—"

"And decent people and opportunities to build something worthwhile," Jonathan finished without heat.

Pushed half by hope and half by fear, my voice shook a little. "You want to chase rainbows."

"You could call it that," he answered coldly.

"Don't think I'll make this offer again, Johnny," the old man fumed. "If you leave *Ombres* now, I want you to know—"

"Will you be all right, Jonathan?" I asked, then added with ill-disguised longing, "Won't you be lonely?"

For the first time he looked directly at me, and even as tired as he was, his eyes were full of rainbows, a lifetime's worth of rainbows. "I won't be if you're there. Come with me, Gene?"

The last time he had held out his hands to me like that, he had given me my life. Now he was doing it again. Ignoring Sebastien's protests and my grandfather's outraged growls, I flew into my beloved's outstretched arms as if that dreadful chasm yawned between us once more, and when he held me close I knew that at last I was where I truly belonged. Wherever we traveled, however we lived, whatever we did, his love would be the only security I would ever need.

About the Author

Janis Susan May is a seventh-generation Texan and a third-generation wordsmith who writes mysteries as Janis Patterson, romances and other things as Janis Susan May, children's books as Janis Susan Patterson and scholarly works as J.S.M. Patterson.

Formerly an actress and singer, a talent agent and Supervisor of Accessioning for a bio-genetic DNA testing lab, Janis has also been editor-in-chief of two multi-magazine publishing groups. She founded and was the original editor of The Newsletter of the North Texas Chapter of the American Research Center in Egypt, which for the nine years of her reign was the international organization's only monthly publication. Long interested in Egyptology, she was one of the founders of the North Texas chapter and was the closing speaker for the ARCE International Conference in Boston in 2005.

Janis married for the first time when most of her contemporaries were becoming grandmothers. Her husband, a handsome Navy Captain several years younger than she, even proposed in a moonlit garden in Egypt. Janis and her husband live in Texas with an assortment of rescued furbabies.

www.JanisSusanMay.com
www.JanisPattersonMysteries.com

CPSIA information can be obtained
at www.ICGtesting.com
Printed in the USA
FFOW04n1356131215
19617FF